Cruising Paradise

———————————————

For John Dark,
my son Jesse,
and days of Garcia y Vega

Cruising Paradise

Tales by
SAM SHEPARD

Secker & Warburg
London

First published in Great Britain in 1996
by Martin Secker & Warburg Limited
an imprint of Reed International Books Limited
Michelin House, 81 Fulham Road, London sw3 6rb
and Auckland, Melbourne, Singapore and Toronto

A CIP catalogue record for this book
is available from the British Library

ISBN 0 436 20333 2

Typeset in 11 on 14 point Baskerville
by Deltatype Limited, Birkenhead, Merseyside
Printed and bound in Great Britain
by Clays Ltd, St Ives plc

'I have a son of yours,' she said to me then. 'There he is.'

And she pointed with her finger at a tall skinny boy with frightened eyes: 'Take off your hat so your father can see you!'

And the boy took off his hat. He was just like me and with something mean in his look. He had to get some of that from his father.

'They call him "El Pichón" too,' the woman, who is now my wife, went on saying. 'But he's not a bandit or a killer. He's a good person.'

I hung my head.

Juan Rulfo

The
Self-Made
Man

For him, it began in a moment of shattering stillness.
Something separated and fell away. Instinctively his heart
understood this 'something' was the long-cherished notion of
himself as a distinct individual; an American entity called
'The Self-Made Man.' He'd learned it through generations
of irascible ancestors with the same hard-set jawline and
gnarly nose. He had pictures of them on his stone mantel.
Tintypes going back to the Civil War of his great-great-
great-grandfather; a man called Lemuel P. Dodge, who lost
an ear fighting for the North, an arm fighting for the South,
and was finally hanged for 'womanizing' in Ojinaga and
dragged through the dusty streets until his head separated
from his torso. There were others: men with long beards and
wide-brimmed straw hats, standing three abreast atop giant
hay wagons, wooden pitchforks in hand, almost biblical
against the prairie sky. Railroad men riding cowcatchers,

waving derbies; blasting their way through granite mountains; unstoppable in their absolute conviction of Manifest Destiny. Then, later generations, where the mysterious glint of doubt begins to creep into their eyes. Fighter pilots in leather helmets and silk scarves, gripping the wings of a P-38, but the brave smile to the camera now has a twist in it, like a lamb knowing his time has come.

He'd study these faces in the evenings sometimes, with the fire glow flickering across the stone mantel. He'd pick up the frames for a closer look and pace the room slowly, smoking and tilting the glass to avoid the glare from the fireplace. He'd sit with the portraits on his lap and dust them softly, lovingly, with his blue bandanna. There was a connection there he felt, more real than imagined. More real than his living relatives, who were now scattered to the far ends of the country: places he had no desire to visit, like Tampa or Seattle. Places that might just as well have been on the other side of the moon. Aloneness was a fact of nature, he reasoned. He'd learned to not look beyond it; to avoid the trickery of the mind where women were concerned; to avoid the imagery of seduction altogether. It had never paid off in the past. The mind was not to be trusted in this regard. It had only led him to terrible sorrow. Now, at least, he'd made some small truce with himself.

He stood up and returned the photo to its place on the mantel: the one of his grandfather driving a Model T pickup with a jack mule in tow. He lingered for a while on the image, listening to the owls feed their young in the top of the old tulip poplar out back. It was a nightly ritual he'd grown to look forward to each spring. He'd take his flashlight, step quietly out onto the porch, and cast its beam up the broad split trunk until he caught the nest in a perfect circle of light. There were two babies this year, and as soon as they felt the light on their eyes, they went silent. The mother hovered above them with a small, black snake in her talons. She turned her back to the beam of light and ruffled her wings, then settled. Spring peepers throbbed into the foreground, replacing the shrieking owls, then receded and dropped away into the distant drone of a semi on its way south. He clicked off the light, hoping the owls would start up their racket again; hoping something would come in to occupy the growing stillness. He listened for calves bawling in the distance. Nothing came. He listened for any sign of wind. Nothing. He cleared his throat to at least hear himself; to feel his own presence there. It sounded to him like a man. Any man. A human without character. As though a stranger had come out on the porch behind him. He turned to look. There was no one. Just his breath. Blood pumping. He was about to speak, but Who to? he thought. Speak what? On whose behalf? His heart picked up, and all his inner language seemed to collect into a pulsing knot at the back of his neck. It burned as though a small black walnut had lodged there and locked his throat shut. Now the panic rushed in. There was no border suddenly between his skin and the night; between his own breath and the surrounding thick air. He turned back to the massive dark tree and looked up. The mother owl's eye blinked down at him. Yellow, then black. His own eye vanished. Emptiness filled him completely. It seemed to rush through him, taking every thought, every feeling. It left nothing behind except the pervasive sense of his own breath. A pulse that he neither originated nor controlled. Peace, he thought, and as quickly as the thought shaped itself, peace left him.

7/16/94 (DEL RIO, TEXAS)

The Real Gabby Hayes

I was seven years old and had driven with my father out to a place on the Mojave called Hot Springs. We'd been looking at a small patch of desert that he'd bought out there from a door-to-door real estate guy who'd spread out glossy color brochures on our kitchen table. Pictures of glistening swimming pools, emerald-green golf courses, and a club-house, all yet to be built. When we got there it was nothing but pure virgin desert. I helped my dad stake his tiny plot with iron rebar on all four corners, tied with little orange flags that snapped in the wind. When we finished, it looked to me more like a cemetery plot than anything else. We spent the rest of the afternoon shooting rusty bean cans with a .22 pistol and looking for snakes. He'd wanted to bring a rattler back with him to show my mother. A green mojave. 'Just to prove we were out here,' he'd said. 'So she doesn't get other ideas. Starts thinking I'm off tomcatting around or something.'

'Is that the reason you brought me along?' I'd said.

'Is what the reason?'

'So she'd think you weren't tomcatting?'

'You're not even sure what tomcattin' means, are you? You're seven years old. How could you be sure what that means?' He turned his back on me and walked away, kicking an empty can and reloading the .22. I could tell he was pissed off for me having asked him that. I followed him, picking up the empty shell casings as they hit the sand. He tossed another can in the air and fired. He missed. He emptied the whole pistol into the sky and missed every time he threw a can. I got embarrassed for him and pretended I hadn't seen this. I found a stick of black manzanita and started drawing diamonds in the sand. He looked over his shoulder at me and reloaded. Sweat was dripping off his nose, and he blew at it as though shooing flies. 'So what's your thought on this little piece of desert here? Think I made a smart deal? The two of us oughta just pick up stakes and move on out here. Just forget about the women altogether.' He laughed and fired again, at a can on the ground. I wasn't sure if he hit it or not, because I wasn't looking, but I didn't hear any metal ring. I was hoping he did hit it, though, because I thought it might help to calm him down some. Get his mind off things. He kept taking long sips from a fifth wrapped in a paper bag that he had stuffed in his hip pocket. He tried to get friendlier with me. I could hear it in his voice. Trying to include me in something, as though I were a conspirator. But the more he tried, the further I felt from him. He seemed to sense this too, but there was nothing he could do about it. 'Sometimes it's good to just get off by yourself someplace. To have a spot like this all tucked away that nobody knows about. Don't you think?' He fired again, at a giant jackrabbit, but didn't come anywhere near it. The rabbit just sat there and stared

at him. 'That's what I had in mind for this place. A little
desert hideaway. Can't always be the family man. Me and
you could build a bottle house out here when you get a little
bit older. What do you think about that?'

'What's a bottle house?' I asked him without looking in
his face.

'You know. A bottle house like these desert rats make.
You seen 'em. All made outa different kinds a bottles,
stacked up like bricks. Different colors. Make a beautiful
light when the sun strikes 'em right.'

'Sure,' I said, still fiddling with the stick.

'Keep a couple a burros. Take hikes and find us some
treasure. There's still treasure out here, ya know. This is
undiscovered territory yet.'

'What kinda treasure?'

'Spanish booty. Cabeza de Vaca musta come right
through here. Ever heard a him? "Head of a Cow" – that's
what his name means. Had a big, ugly head, apparently.
From all the accounts. I'll bet he came right through here,
searching for Cibola.'

'What's that?'

'Seven Cities of Gold. You'll learn all about that when
you start your history. You haven't started on any history
yet, I guess.'

'No. Just dinosaurs.'

'Well, this was way after the dinosaurs. This was when the
Spanish had this notion that there was a place made entirely
of gold. I don't know where the idea came from, but they
were convinced it was out here in the West somewhere.'

'Did they ever find it?'

'Nope. But old de Vaca had a Negro man – a Moor I
guess they called them back then. Big, giant Negro man that
de Vaca used as his scout. He'd send him out in search of
the golden cities, and one day this Negro came back to

6

camp and told de Vaca he'd finally found it. So they rushed to this place with the Moor leading the way and when they got there it turned out to be a Pueblo Indian village carved into the side of a cliff. When the sun hit the pueblo at a certain time of day, it appeared to be golden. So de Vaca had the Moor beheaded.'

'Beheaded?'

'Yep. Chopped his head right off. On the spot.' My dad walked away, leaving me with the image of decapitation. A horny toad blinked right in front of me. I never would have noticed him if he hadn't blinked. 'Anyhow, this would be the perfect kind of spot for a little hideaway. Just the two of us.'

'You mean we'd just live out here by ourselves?' I asked him.

'Well, not permanent. Not on a permanent basis. Just have it as a kind of a retreat. Nobody'd know about it except you and me. Be our little secret. Have to bring water to it, of course. That's the chief problem out here, is water. We could haul it in from Indio, I suppose. Dig a well.'

'We'd never bring Mom?' This question seemed to piss him off again. He kicked at the sand and spun the chamber of the pistol.

'She's not the desert type,' he said. 'Forests is her game. Woods and lakes. Midwestern stuff.' He fired into an old kerosene can that was so close he couldn't miss. 'She likes it where it's all closed in and you can't see the light of day. Not my cup a tea. Bottle house would be perfect. All those different shafts of colored light.'

We drove across the sand, back to the blacktop highway, and stopped at a Date Shack advertising *Date Shakes* in gigantic hand-painted red letters. He asked the Mexican owner for directions to a place called the Shadow Mountain Inn – some kind of country club he'd remembered from his air force days. We shared a box of dates stuffed with coconut shavings, and he kept licking his fingers and saying, 'Beats the hell out of a Hershey bar!' We found our way to the Shadow Mountain Inn and parked right in front of it. He wrapped the .22 up in an old racing form, then stuffed it under the front seat. He took one more long hit from his bottle and hid that in the glove compartment underneath some yellowed highway maps. I started feeling as though I should be hiding something too, but I wasn't sure what it was.

As we crossed the parking lot he told me this was a very exclusive club and we should act like we belonged here. It never occurred to me before that 'acting' could be a part of living. 'It's all in the way you present yourself,' he said. 'If you go in there acting like you don't belong, like you feel awkward or something, they're gonna sense that right off the bat. Just act natural and relaxed, like a solid citizen.'

We sat at the mahogany bar, and my dad ordered a martini with white pearl onions floating around in it. He pulled a big bowl of peanuts over and placed it between us. I thought the peanuts might belong to somebody else, since they were already set out, but he dug right into them. I'd never seen him order a martini before, but I guess he was trying to impress the bartender. Back home he'd always order bourbon and soda. I got a cherry Coke with a slice of lemon, and it was right about then, when the Coke was delivered, that I saw Gabby Hayes. The real Gabby Hayes. At first I couldn't believe it. I kept staring to make sure before I said anything to my dad. I was hypnotized by his white beard. There he was, big as life, sitting in a plush corner booth with a black string bolo tie and a shiny tuxedo. It was the middle of a desert afternoon, about 109 degrees outside, so hot the blacktop was melting, and Gabby Hayes had on a tuxedo. There were two young blond women with him, decked out in slinky cocktail outfits, dripping with jewelry and sex. Even at seven, I could recognize sex when I saw it. There was no mistake about that. They kept dangling shrimp dipped in red sauce in front of his nose, giggling and nibbling on his fuzzy ears. One of them had her hand in his lap under a white linen napkin. 'Dad, that's Gabby Hayes over there! The real Gabby Hayes!' I whispered heavily. My heart was banging for some reason, and my breath came out choppy and dry. My father turned stiffly on his stool, and I could smell the boozy sweat on the back of his sunburned neck. He glanced over at the corner booth and then turned back to his drink.

'That's what fame and fortune'll get you,' he said. 'Couple a blond chippies and a shrimp cocktail. How 'bout that.' I kept staring at Gabby Hayes's beard and watching his mouth nibble on the shrimp, then suck on the girl's finger. It looked like he had a whole set of ivory-white teeth now. On TV he never had teeth. On TV he never wore a tuxedo. He was the subservient gummy-mouthed sidekick, slightly demented and always shy around women. It never crossed my mind that the real Gabby Hayes might be a whole different person.

That night we drove all the way back home in silence. My dad smoked and squinted down the long road toward the lights of Duarte. He turned the radio on once and listened to Frank Sinatra sing 'You Belong to Me,' then turned it back off again. I stared out at the dark string of mountains that diminished behind us into the deep desert, and above them I saw a huge decapitated head of a black man smiling down on us.

3/11/90 (PAPANTLA, MEXICO)

Nuevo Mundo

(first told to Arnold R. Rojas)

In the late 1850s, Perfecto Cuen was a young man of fifteen. He had already acquired the basic skills with a rawhide reata and enough of the art of la jineta to be known amongst his peers as a true vaquero. He had made the long journey south on horseback through the great San Joaquin Valley to the settlement of Los Angeles, where he'd heard the Mormons were buying up large herds of cattle to make drives back to their colony in Utah. He was hired on as a hand, along with several gringo sailors who had jumped ship and were looking toward the cattle drive as a means of getting themselves back east. How sailors transformed themselves into horsemen was something Perfecto never asked out loud. He was a gentleman from the silent paisano tradition of his Sonoran ancestors.

After delivering the herd safely to the Mormons, Perfecto was paid off in a solid gold bar, said adiós to the saddle-sore sailors, and pointed his mustang back toward California. His mind was racing with notions of how he would spend his booty wildly in the cantinas of San Luis Obispo. Already, slender date palms were swaying before him, and he had days in the saddle before he'd reach them.

He crossed the parched white ocean of sand, saving his horse and picking his way carefully, making note of any faint signs of water: signs he'd learned through the viejos and brujas of his homeland. He traveled by moonlight to protect himself and his mount from the raging, merciless sun. Always, in the back of his mind, was the brotherhood of his vaquero culture, which prodded him on. He could see the hawklike faces of the old ones telling their cuentos in the campfire circle. Guitars, the sweat of horseflesh, and cracked leather. These camps were home to him. These small bands of nomadic horsemen descended from Moors, Yaqui, and the Spanish conquistadores.

As he entered eastern Nevada, he came across an Indian encampment. He carried none of the white man's apprehension in this encounter, as the natives of that region were very friendly toward Spanish-speaking men and never molested their cattle or horses. Vaqueros were free to come and go as they pleased, and it was on this occasion that Perfecto discovered the reason why. The headmen of the tribe presented him with several documents they'd been issued by the original Spaniards, who'd invaded that country decades before. These Indians still considered themselves allies or subjects of Spain and, to them, Perfecto was a member of the ruling class and, therefore, honored and revered. Perfecto tried to explain that he could neither read nor write, but he did recognize the seals and rubricas accompanying the ancient signature at the bottom of each page. The Indians would stab the parchment with their dark fingers and assure him that these declarations would guarantee him safe passage across their sacred lands. Perfecto, with all the graciousness a fifteen-year-old could muster up, removed his wide sombrero and paid tribute to an empire long since powerless to enforce its decrees in this new world. The Indians were duly impressed by the young man's fidelity to the Crown and beseeched him to stay with them and take a wife. Any wife. He could have his pick of the entire village. Bands of prickly sweat began to break out across Perfecto's chest. He knew that to refuse their offer would be a horrible insult. An insult that could easily result in death, regardless of the sanctified documents. Besides, he had a saddlebag loaded heavy with gold to spend in the verdant streets of San Luis Obispo. He also knew that to accept a wife here would mean he would never be allowed to escape, in spite of his expert horsemanship. They would track him and find him. They would track him clear to California if they had to.

Perfecto dismounted slowly, his mind crashing between the two impossible alternatives. As the spiked rowels of his Spanish spurs jingled beneath him, he felt as though he would suddenly pass out and never return to this earth; never see his beloved homeland again. He was shown to a tepee, and many young girls were paraded before him, all giggling and fluttering their eyes. The chief decided to hasten the proceedings and pulled one of the ripest and youngest from the line. He placed the girl in front of Perfecto and ran his scarred hands slowly across her full, naked breasts. He grinned and nodded at Perfecto, but Perfecto only stared at the bleached-out ground in front of him. His sombrero was in his hands. His mouth was drier than it had ever been on any desert crossing. His heart was pounding with a fear he'd never felt before. All the weary miles he'd covered on the spiny back of his little mustang gelding, picking his way through terrible snake-infested country punctured by cholla cactus, dying for the candles of home… And now, here, he would face his death, he thought.

Here, in the hands of a strange primitive generosity he wanted no part of.

The chief left them alone and ushered off the remaining girls. Their giggling and whooping diminished into the coming night. The girl stared at Perfecto, but he wouldn't look up, wouldn't look her in the eyes. He was weeping now but making no sound. Only his shoulders twitched slightly, with the grief that knotted through his stomach and the back of his throat. The salty tears rolled down into the corners of his mouth and tasted as brackish as the little water he'd found in the Great Salt Desert of Utah. He could see his death before him. It appeared on the ground as a headless snake: a shadow, growing, then receding into light; the head joining the body, then breaking off again and diving deep inside the black earth. He was afraid to move. Afraid his spurs would rattle and give the girl some new idea. The chill of the night was setting in, and his whole body began to quiver. The girl must have noticed this and went to his horse to retrieve his poncho. She brought it back to him and covered his shoulders with it. She saw the stripes of his tears and licked his cheeks with her rough tongue. Her tongue reminded him of a young calf's, sucking on his fingers when he'd get an orphan started on a nurse cow. Perfecto never looked up from the ground. He kept his eyes pinned on his death, right there in front of him. The girl backed away and sat down softly. Although she was completely naked, she never showed any signs of the cold. She stared up at him, but he wouldn't let her see his eyes. All through the night they remained like that: her sitting opposite him; Perfecto standing stock-still. She would sigh now and then, making a light, feathery sound and clacking her teeth, then go silent again. He prayed without moving his lips. Prayed to his guardian saint to deliver him from all sin. Sins he may have forgotten. Sins he may have committed without knowing.

Sins of the mind and the body. The girl stood up and moved to the entrance of the tepee, sweeping her thick black hair from side to side as though invoking him to follow. Perfecto remained. He stood there through the night, draped in his poncho, head bent, and holding his sombrero in both hands.

When the chief found him like that in the first rays of the sunrise, he understood that this was a man of true power. This was no mere boy. He must have been sent to his people by the Spanish Crown itself as some kind of omen. He agreed to let Perfecto pass on to his homeland without malice, and as the vaquero mounted his scrawny little mustang, the girl came running toward him. She clutched at his tapaderos and spurs, trying to pull his boots from the stirrups. She threw herself to the ground at the feet of his horse and began clawing her breasts. An animal scream came from her that sent ice through Perfecto's spine, but he never looked down at her. He urged his horse toward the Sierras and kept his eyes on the blue horizon. All the girls in the camp were laughing and prodding the one on the ground. The one in agony. They dragged her to her feet and goaded her to follow the rider. The girl chased him for miles, screaming like a wild dog and pulling her hair out. Perfecto never looked back or changed the pace of his horse. He had eyes only for California.

7/13/94 (DEL RIO, TEXAS)

Days of Blackouts

1943:

The Office of War Mobilization is invented.
Eisenhower is made Supreme Commander of all Allied forces.
Mussolini resigns.
My dad is dropping bombs on Italy.
I'm born
Without a clue.

1943:

There's a little motor court on the outskirts of Mountain Home, Idaho. Through some secret code system my father has worked out on postcards with my mother, she deciphers the exact room number and time to meet him. (No bomber pilot is supposed to reveal his itinerary to even the closest blood relative.) This motor court is laid out in the shape of a horseshoe, with all the identical bungalow units surrounding a shallow concrete fish pond, glowing a pale green from a floodlight submerged in the middle of it. There are two metal lawn chairs facing the pond, underneath a pair of white pines. My mother sits on one of them in a Hawaiian flower-print dress that she brought back from the Philippines when we were stationed over there. She has a pink hibiscus in her jet-black hair, and she's leaning forward, elbows on her knees, smiling down at the swimming fish. She has a flirtatious, teenage smile, which I notice even though I can't speak any language yet and have no control over my bowels. My father sits in the other chair in his khaki uniform and leather brimmed flight cap. I'm on his knee, staring down into the shimmering green light of the pond. The air is very still and smells like pine, and there's stars thick through the whole sky.

1943:

'You'd Be So Nice to Come Home To'
'Don't Get Around Much Anymore'
'That Old Black Magic Has Me in Its Spell'
'Comin' in on a Wing and a Prayer'

1943:

My mother is pointing to a yellow fish and tracking it with her finger, trying to get me to notice – this one particular fish with a long flowing tail. 'Like a bird!' she says in a sweet voice, full of wonder. 'It's almost like a bird! See? There it goes!' My father leans forward, and I can feel the metal chair uncoil beneath him, then settle back again in a series of descending ripples. His bristly cheek brushes mine as he stares down into the green water, and his silver wings and air force medals burrow into my back. A sudden rush of cold air from the mountains takes my breath away.

1943:

Shoe rationing.
Meat rationing.
Cheese rationing.
No butter.
Roosevelt declares a 48-hour workweek.
The German army surrenders to the Russians.

1943:

My mother is getting more and more excited about this fish. She's down on her knees now on the grass, leaning across the pond, pointing and giggling, throwing her hair back out of her face. The pink hibiscus goes flying from her head and sails right past my eyes. My father makes a lunge for it and loses me. Now I'm airborne, flying toward the shiny pond and the falling hibiscus. I'm suspended, watching the flower touch down softly on the surface without sinking, and twirling like a ballerina, just before I crash into the rippling green light. My blanket is floating beside me.

1943:

Race riots in Detroit, L.A., Mobile, Harlem, and Beaumont, Texas.
Count Fleet wins the Triple Crown.
James Cagney is 'Yankee Doodle Dandy.'

1943:

My father is having a nightmare on one of the twin beds in the bungalow of the motor court in Mountain Home, Idaho.

I'm sleeping in the bottom drawer of the dresser that's been pulled out on a throw rug. My mother is quietly taking a shower. My blanket is drying by the window. I can hear it dripping. My father is seeing bombs raining on Italy. He sees these bombs diminishing beneath him. Falling away from his sweaty feet toward the 'boot' of Italy. He sees the hand-painted cartoon faces on these bombs: detailed cartoon devils; demons; diminishing. Falling away. He sees his own white hand stretching out the cockpit window, desperately clutching; trying to catch these painted monster cartoon creatures before they smash the blank face of Italy.

1943:

Rachmaninoff dies.
Streptomycin is isolated.
Jackson Pollock has his first one-man show.
God Is My Co-Pilot hits the best-seller list.

I'm born
Without a clue.

5/94 (CHICAGO)

Wild
to the
Wild

This was in the days when you could still mail-order wild baby animals from ads in the back of hunting and fishing magazines, like *Field and Stream*. You just sent away for them with your check or money order, and a month or so later they'd arrive, snarling and spitting in a wooden crate, down at the train depot. My friend Mitchell Chaney, who played slide trombone in our three-piece combo at high school, had collected almost every wild baby animal available at the time. (Nobody'd ever heard of an 'endangered species.') I'd gone in with him on a couple of the cheaper ones, like the baby alligator and the baby armadillo, for instance. They were all kept at Mitchell's place, though, because we had too many dogs at ours and my dad was a firm believer in leaving the wild to the wild.

Evenings, when we'd rehearse our band over at Mitchell's, we'd go out in his backyard and make the rounds, checking all the cages, making sure the water and feed tanks were full, hosing out the messes they'd made (especially the spider monkey), and adding strands of coat-hanger wire to the mesh on the wolf pup's trapdoor. We couldn't find wire thick enough to keep him in. It would take him two or three days, but he'd eventually chew right through it, sometimes leaving a bloody tooth dangling behind. Then he'd end up wandering around on the railroad tracks that bordered Mitchell's backyard, killing chickens and rooting through the neighborhood garbage. We had a hell of a time catching him, too, trying to bait him with raw hot dogs and then dragging him back with a tow chain borrowed from Mitchell's dad. He was getting to be a good size now – about sixty pounds and pure muscle. The Union Pacific ran a fruit train through town about six o'clock every evening, and we were both well aware of the deadline for getting our wolf out of its path.

Nat Henkins, our clarinet player, was not into the wild baby animal thing like me and Mitchell were. It just didn't interest him for some reason. In fact, the only thing that seemed to twirl Nat's ticket was forties big band music. The Dorsey Brothers and that ilk. He modeled himself after the young Benny Goodman, parting his hair straight down the middle and slicked back with pomade; he wore heavy black-rimmed glasses and kept his top button buttoned at all times. He also read sheet music fluently, which kept me and Mitchell somewhat in a state of awe, although privately we thought he was a dipshit. He was the only clarinet player in school, though, so we had to make do. Of the three of us, Nat looked the most out of place trying to pull a wolf pup off the railroad tracks. His body never looked fully committed to the task. Neither did his clothes. He would rest too long between pulls and spend a lot of time wiping the palms of his hands on his pants and staring vacantly down the tracks. His hands were extremely white and long-fingered, with milky, soft

J|45 9244

nails. The groans he made when he pulled on the chain were full of complaint rather than true effort, and this started to piss me and Mitchell off. We could sense Nat's halfhearted-ness and lack of urgency. Mitchell's voice was punctuated by gasps for air as he leaned against the weight of the baby wolf: 'You understand, Nat, that the fruit train is gonna be blasting through here in about fifteen minutes? You understand that, don't you? We gotta get this wolf off the tracks!'

'It never blasts through,' Nat said. 'That's an exaggera-tion. They're not allowed to blast through towns. It's a law. They have to slow down when they see civilization. Besides, I don't see why you don't just turn him loose. Wolf's not gonna just stand here and let himself get smashed by a fruit train. He's not that stupid.'

Mitchell stopped pulling and stood up straight, staring hard into Nat's lean face. 'He's a wild animal, Nat. It's got nothing to do with "stupid." He's wild. He's never seen a train before in his life. He doesn't know about trains.'

'Doesn't mean he's gonna let himself get creamed by one. He hears the noise and the whistle, he'll run. It's a natural instinct.' Nat's levelheadedness only seemed to fire Mitchell's anger.

'I've got the feeling you could give a shit about the fate of our baby wolf, Nat.'

'I'm just sick of wasting all this time when we could be practicing. Every time I come over, you guys are always messing around with these dumb animals. It takes us forever to get started.'

'So you wanna just turn him loose and let him get hit by a train or a car or run off in the hills and die somewhere?'

'He's not gonna die in the hills. He's a wolf, for Christ's sake.'

The pup just sat there with his hocks dug into the gravel, panting and drooling on the rail, his tongue darting in and out

like a pink lizard. I dropped the chain and sat down on the cold rail beside the pup. The wolf's breath smelled like raw hot dogs and cottage cheese, which was exactly what we'd been feeding him. I stared into his yellow eyes and saw that he had no recognition of me in the way that my dogs did. He wasn't expecting anything from me, like a pat or a handout. He was in a world of his own. His head looked suddenly huge, like the close-ups of King on *Sergeant Preston of the Yukon.*

'What're we gonna do with this wolf, Mitchell, when he gets full-grown?' I asked, without taking my eyes off the pup. 'Did you ever think of that?'

'We're gonna breed him. There's a huge market for hybrids.' Nat snickered and shook his head hopelessly at the ground. He pulled a pressed handkerchief out of his back pocket and started cleaning his glasses, holding them up to the fading sky, then breathing little clouds of fog on the lenses and rubbing in rapid flurries like he'd seen older men do. Mature men. Like his father, maybe, or his uncle. I suddenly saw that the difference between me and Nat lay in some hidden, secret pattern that had nothing to do with who we thought we were. Patterns of belief and behavior that accrued to us imperceptibly through the men we were growing up with. Men we took to be legitimate and irrefutable. 'We're gonna breed him to one of your sheep dogs,' Mitchell continued, but it was directed more toward Nat, as some kind of vague challenge.

'Which one?' I said.

'Whichever one's in heat. You can have pick of the litter.'

Nat kept rubbing his glasses and squinting down at them as he spoke. 'When're you guys ever gonna have time to rehearse? You'll be running a zoo here pretty soon. You gotta make up your minds what line of work you're gonna follow in this life. You wanna be musicians or wolf breeders?' It was this smugness about Nat that drew me and

Mitchell into a tighter camaraderie. This 'philosophical' tone of his: using 'this life' as though it would put us in our place; as though 'this life' was up ahead of us somewhere and had nothing to do with trains or wolves or the waning light. Mitchell hunkered down on the tracks beside me, with our stubborn wolf between us, as Nat continued his little sermon: 'You guys don't seem to realize it takes work to make a band. Years of dedicated work. It's got to be the first thing on your list. We can't even get straight through "Old Black Magic" without making mistakes.'

'I hate "Old Black Magic," to tell you the truth,' Mitchell said as he tossed a chunk of gravel at the iron rail. 'Stupid lyrics. "Those icy fingers up and down my spine. That same old witchcraft when your eyes meet mine." What kinda corny horseshit is that?'

'We're not playing the lyrics,' Nat said. 'That's not the point. It doesn't matter what the lyrics are. We're playing the tune. You hate the Peggy Lee version, but I've been trying to tell you we aren't trying to imitate the Peggy Lee version.'

'What are we trying to imitate, then?' I asked.

'It's not a question of imitation,' Nat persisted. 'It's more like laying a foundation. We can't just develop our own style out of thin air.'

'Why not?' Mitchell said.

'Because that's not the way it happens!' Nat got more agitated with his handkerchief-rubbing. 'We have to memorize the old standards. We gotta get those down so well we could do them in our sleep. "Blue Moon," "Down by the Old Mill Stream" – stuff like that. Classics. Then we can start to innovate and develop our own sound. It's a slow evolution. That's how a band gets born.'

'Well, I'm sick of that forties shit,' Mitchell said as he grazed the rail with another chunk of gravel. The wolf pricked his ears at the high stinging sound, then rolled over on his side and kept up his rapid panting.

'I think we oughta try some improvising,' I said. 'What's the point of memorizing the standards if we're never gonna play 'em? We never play them at the sock hops.'

'Because it gives us a background to build on. A foundation,' Nat said. 'We're not gonna play sock hops forever. Without the basics, we're just fishing in the dark. How do you think all the greats got started? Ellington, Count Basie, the Dorseys? You think they just started improvising wildly, hoping for the best?'

'We're a three-piece outfit, not a goddamn orchestra!' Mitchell exploded. 'If you wanna do some classic stuff, then let's do something like 'Madagascar,' not 'Satin Doll' and 'Old Black Magic.' That's for old farts.'

'Who did "Madagascar"?' Nat asked, genuinely mystified, and Mitchell turned to me and smiled. I don't know why he smiled, because I'd never heard of the tune either.

'Wilbur De Paris,' Mitchell said, turning smugly back to Nat.

'Who the fuck's Wilbur De Paris?' I said, and Mitchell snapped his head toward me like I'd betrayed some deep pact between us.

'New Orleans,' Mitchell said, trying to give it an esoteric drift. 'My dad's got it in his collection. I'll play it for you when we get back to the house.'

'I don't know,' I said. 'I like the Chicago guys myself. That's about all I can listen to anymore. Beats the stew outa Perry Como anyhow.'

'Like who?' Nat said. 'Like who from Chicago?'

'Like J. B. Lenoir, that's who,' I said.

'What'd he do?'

' "Eisenhower Blues"?'

' "Eisenhower Blues"?'

'Yeah, "Eisenhower Blues." '

'That's obscure,' Nat said. 'You wanna be obscure, or do you wanna develop into a real band?'

'I wanna be a veterinarian!' I said. And that shut Nat up for the rest of the time. He got so depressed and silent he just wandered off away from us, with his glasses dangling from his left hand and his head drooped way down into his chest. His feet slipped going down the gravel bank of the tracks, and he picked himself up without even brushing off his slacks. Me and Mitchell never laughed at him, though. We felt kind of bad for him in his disappointment, but we didn't call out to bring him back or try to make things better for him. It was best he faced the music on his own. We watched him walk away, back to Mitchell's yard, and go through the broken iron gate without trying to close it behind him. He never looked back at us. He just kept walking down the driveway and out onto the street. As he hit the sidewalk, the bluish streetlamps all came on at the same time, as though triggered by his footstep.

The six o'clock fruit train moaned in the distance, and the crossings were clanging through town, all the way out to Fish Canyon. The wolf pup jumped up and pricked his ears, then shook himself the way a horse does, where the shiver travels from the neck down the backbone and out through the tail. Not like a domestic dog, who shakes himself all in one piece. He stopped panting and stared in the direction of the oncoming train. He gave a little whine, then turned and loped off away from us down the track, dragging the chain behind him. Me and Mitchell just stood and watched him run off into the night. We never even called out to him. He didn't know his name anyhow.

5/2/89 (SCOTTSVILLE, VIRGINIA)

A
Man's
Man

One fine morning at breakfast, my dad announced that he'd lined me up a job working at a horse ranch out in Chino. He'd gone out of his way to arrange this through my 4-H Club leader, Duane McFiel, a huge Scotsman with hands the size of catcher's mitts. He was a 'man's man,' according to my father; a man not afraid of hard work, and the implication was that I, too, could become such a man just by way of association. Duane was to pick me up at 5:30 a.m. the next morning in his '57 Chevy and drive me out to Chino to show me the ropes. Five-thirty was an auspicious time to rise, my father told me, because it was the hour when more animals were born and more crimes of passion were committed. I was tempted to ask him what the link was between passionate crime and animal birth, but this was the type of question my father absolutely could not tolerate, so I let it go.

Duane McFiel's '57 Chevy coupe was the kind of car

every guy in high school would have killed for. Jet black with slick chrome trim, shark fins, and the lightning-quick short-block V-8 that made Chevy famous on the back streets of America. Duane made no bones about showing it off to me either. From the moment he picked me up in the driveway, clear across the wasteland of San Bernardino County, he was stomping down on it, burning rubber at every empty inter-section and nailing the tachometer into the red zone. He'd grin like a kid and cackle and pat the steering wheel like he would a good old hunting dog. This was my 4-H Club leader, who, up till then, I'd seen only in the role of reserved instructor, giving little lectures with color charts and a pointing stick on the details of butchering a feeder steer. Now he'd suddenly transformed into a slightly manic teenage street dragster.

As we finally approached the ranch, he began to caution me about how to handle myself on this new job of mine. I wasn't to ask any questions about the operation to anyone. The owners were some kind of anonymous Mormon organization, who raced Thoroughbreds under a bogus stable moniker. As a matter of fact, they'd just won the Kentucky Derby, against all odds, with a horse named Swaps, but I wasn't even supposed to let on about this. 'Don't even mention it to your father,' Duane warned. His voice took on this clandestine aura as we pulled up to the steel gates, wrapped with a huge chain and padlock. There was nothing fancy about the place. Just barbed-wire-and-steel-pipe corral. No little statuettes of jockeys in their colors, holding rings. Nothing at all to indicate the glitz and glamour of horse racing. 'They've got this tough old Arizona cowboy as their trainer and foreman. You might see him riding around the alfalfa fields on a big stout sorrel horse. Don't look at him or say anything to him. Just pretend he's not even there.'

'He's the boss?' I asked.

'He's the boss. You might have seen him on the cover of *Life*. He's the one who rode in a boxcar with Swaps all the way out there to Kentucky for the Derby. Sat right there in a corner of the boxcar with a shotgun laid across his lap. Said he wanted to make sure nobody tried to dope his horse or steal it. Kind of a crazy old bugger, if you ask me, but he's definitely the boss.'

As we entered the outfit, the tule fog was so thick I couldn't make out the paddocks and barns; I could just see a long corridor of sandy narrow ranch road, skirted with barbed wire. 'Where's all the horses?' I asked Duane.

'Don't you worry about the livestock. That's not any of our concern. We're here to buck hay, and that's the extent of it.' We kept knifing slowly through the thick fog to the back side of the ranch, where I could begin to make out trim rows of square-baled alfalfa, awaiting our muscle. There was already a flatbed and crew out there, creeping along the line of bales with its pale orange lights bleeding through the mist. The sap went out of my body at the thought of wrestling those one-hundred-fifty-pound three-wire bales for the whole rest of the day.

I started out stacking on the back of the flatbed, as the driver inched through the field and Duane tossed those bales at me from the ground. You had to be quick enough to keep ahead of him; placing each bale bricklike and tight, then turning back fast enough not to catch the next one directly in the chest. One slip of your hay hooks, and the next bale was already on top of you. I'd been hit by one of those suckers before, and it was like a tree had dropped across me. Duane was a gorilla man. The harder he worked, the stronger he got. He seemed to enjoy the punishment, grinning up at me with each heave and cackling like he did in the Chevy. Between swings he'd sometimes snap one thumb to his nostril and blow white snot out the other. He reminded me of one of those giant red-headed Scotsmen throwing timbers at the Highland Games. And I was on the receiving end. The sockets in my shoulders already felt dislocated, and the day'd only just begun.

On our first break, the fog was starting to rise and across the back fenceline I could hear dozens of male voices shouting out numbers in cadence. In the bar of light between the ground and fog I could make out rows of gray legs springing back and forth in calisthenic rhythm. 'Chino State Prison,' Duane told me as he crunched into a Hershey bar. 'Merle Haggard's supposed to be in there. Got arrested for stealing his uncle's car. Imagine that: your own uncle has you thrown in the pen. Times have changed, I guess.' On the far end of the long hayfield, a horseman suddenly broke through the fog and reined to a stop. He just stood there, watching us from a distance with both hands crossed on the saddle horn and kind of leaning in our direction as though studying a herd of cattle. 'That's him!' Duane said as he bolted off the flatbed and snatched up his hay hooks. 'That's the man! Let's go!' The driver, an older man in his sixties, hustled back into the cab of the truck and fired it up. I stood slowly, trying to unbend my aching spine, and watched the horseman out across the wet, flat field. He nudged his gray western hat back off his forehead, then returned his hand to the saddle horn and kept right on staring at us. I couldn't make out his eyes, but I wondered right then what it was about certain men that caused other men to panic. 'Let's go, let's go!' Duane was yelling up at me. 'Grab your hooks! Get with it now!'

We finished the day at sundown, and I remember sinking into the red upholstery of Duane's car thinking I'd never be able to walk again. 'Not a bad day's work once you get into the rhythm of it.' Duane chortled. 'It's all mental anyhow.'

As we made our way back out the sandy road, a chestnut stallion came blowing up to us on the other side of the fence, as though challenging the car. He flared his nostrils and shook his head at us.

'That's not Swaps, is it?' I asked Duane.

'Could be. That very well could be the horse. Acts like a racehorse, doesn't he?'

'That's the horse that just won the Kentucky Derby? I can't believe it!'

'Sure looks like him to me. Let's see what kind of speed he's got.' Duane floored the V-8, getting a jump on the stallion, then, before the transmission could kick into second, the horse went flying by us like we were standing still. It was so effortless and fluid he reminded me of a leopard more than a horse. Duane turned to me with his eyebrows raised clear back to his hairline. 'Goddamn! That's got to be Swaps!' He broke out in hysterical fits of laughter, slapping the steering wheel and shaking his head. 'We just got our butt kicked by Swaps! Imagine that!' I'd temporarily lost all sense of fatigue and soreness, and craned my neck around to get a glimpse of the incredible animal as we passed him at the paddock corner. He kept shaking his head at us and stomping the earth as though daring us to try it again. 'I never heard of a horse beating a Chevy before, have you? That's gotta be a first!'

I fell into a deep comatose sleep somewhere on the outskirts of Riverside and didn't wake up until I discovered Duane's huge hand resting on my crotch. It was just laying there limp, like a piece of raw hamburger. 'You're home,' he said, and returned his hand to the steering wheel with a meek smile that made me suddenly sorry for him.

As I walked up the driveway toward the house, I could see my dad in the light of the kitchen, fixing a drink. He was in a T-shirt, and his head slumped down toward his chest. He raised his face toward the ceiling, then turned to the window and stared out in my direction. I knew he couldn't see me because the yard light was blown, but I stopped anyway and waited. My whole body ached, and all I wanted was to crash in my bed, but I couldn't move. I waited for the longest time, just watching him stare out the window, hoping he'd leave the kitchen so I wouldn't have to pass him on the way in. It was pitch-black outside; no cars on the road; not one dog barked. I couldn't even see the moon. I kept waiting for him to turn the light out and leave the kitchen, but he just kept standing there and staring. What was going through his head? Was he waiting for me? I felt this panic start to boom up through my chest and ears. This old familiar fear. What was it about certain men?

5/18/95 (SCOTTSVILLE, VIRGINIA)

Packing

Packing always brought on a nausea to him. That little faint
tickle at the top of the throat. The cotton mouth. Just the
sight of his underwear and socks waiting for him blankly on
the chair. The stack of faded T-shirts. He didn't care what
order his clothes went into the green duffel. He jammed
them in at random and never thought about what he might
need first or what town he might be stopping in on the very
first night. In fact, he had no notion now of which direction
to take or what highway. It was a coin toss. He tried to
picture a destination: Lexington; El Paso; Boulder City. He
had no idea. They all ran together. He tried to see himself
being there. Somewhere. Arriving. Albuquerque, maybe.
Tucumcari. He saw a Denny's coffee shop that seemed
familiar, right across from a playground and an old railroad
station; but he couldn't be sure which town he remembered
them from or why these places would give him any reason to
return. He thought about burning all his maps.

It was dark now as he moved into the bathroom and gathered up his toothbrush and electric shaver. He couldn't believe it was dark again. He'd slept clear through the day; maybe fifteen hours or more. The kind of sleep that leaves you weak and deathlike. His legs felt like they were filled with Silly Putty. He still hadn't eaten. Maybe he'd just stop off at the Happy Chef on his way out of town and get a patty melt. He needed something. He had a destination now.

He returned to his packing but found himself utterly lost in the midst of an action; standing numbly by the shower, with the shaver dangling from his hand; turning toward the mirror like he'd forgotten something. Something he couldn't remember. He caught a quick glimpse of his face staring back at him. His gaunt, ungiving face. His eyes jerked away as though there were some shame involved. Some shame of being totally devoid of purpose. He shook it off and went doggedly toward his duffel, parked on the bed. He marched toward it like he'd just received some order to 'snap out of it.' He dumped the shaver and toothbrush in, then zipped it up. It was the first really satisfying sensation he'd had since he'd awoken – the sound of the zipper engaging its green teeth, without a snag. He turned and looked around the motel room again, searching for some item he might have overlooked. It was just an old habit that he remembered from his mother, back when the two of them used to chase his father from one air force base to another. Back in the days of motor courts. She'd take him by the hand, after they'd thrown the luggage in the huge trunk of their Plymouth coupe, and the two of them would search every inch of the room for something they might have forgotten; he never knew what. They'd open every drawer of every dresser, every cabinet, even ones they never used, and his mother would run her hand back into the corners and down along the edges, sometimes taking the drawer out completely and turning it upside down until the yellowing newspaper that lined the bottom floated out to the floor. Then she'd shake the naked drawer above her head and peer up into it until she was completely satisfied it wasn't holding some personal treasure of hers, like a bobby pin. Then they'd check every closet, walking all the way into them and turning on the bare bulb. He remembered looking up at her white arms as she ran the empty hangers back and forth on the pipe poles until they chimed. They'd search the bathroom, and she'd climb right into the tub with her high heels on and pick up the little rectangles of mushy soap and peek underneath them. 'I lost your father's ring this way, once,' she'd said as she ran her red thumbnail along the rippled base of a soap dish. 'I'd taken it off while I was soaking in the tub and put it in a soap dish, just like this one. When I put the soap back on top of it, the ring buried right into it, and I couldn't find it for a week. I thought I was going to die. I couldn't tell your father about it, and I kept having to hide my ring hand from him all the time. I was so ashamed. I finally found it in a wastepaper basket. I don't know how in the world it got in there. Can you imagine? Your father never even suspected it was missing. I don't know what I'd have done if he'd noticed it wasn't on my hand. That's why it's important to check very thoroughly before you pay your bill. You can't blame someone for stealing if you leave things behind.'

7/91 (KADOKA, SOUTH DAKOTA)

Cruising
Paradise

Crewlaw's dad had burned himself up in a motel bed. That was the story. Mattress exploded or something. The details kept bothering me. Crewlaw told me the cause of it was a big cigar ember that had flopped off while his dad was unconscious; drunk. The ember had rolled down his T-shirt, found its way to the sheets, and burned clear through the mattress, causing internal combustion. I couldn't quite picture it, although Crewlaw related it as though he'd been a witness to the whole event. He got personally insulted that I wasn't getting it, and took the attitude that I thought he was lying to me, which I knew he wasn't. He said he'd take me over to the motel where it happened and show me the mattress itself, if I didn't believe him. I told him I *did* believe him, I just couldn't picture it, but he dragged me out there anyway.

We drove out to Azusa on Highway 66 in Crewlaw's '48 Mercury with gray-primered skirts and parked in a gravel lot beside the Jupiter Motel, one of those quasi-Spanish-stucco courtyard jobs with a dead fountain in the middle and no customers. Crewlaw leaned way across me and pointed to a dark back window with some kind of red decal slapped across a corner, advertising *Overhead Cams*. I could smell his Butchwax and the Lucky Strikes rolled up in the sleeve of his T-shirt. 'That's where it happened,' he said. 'Right there. See that window?'

'What was he doing way out here?'

'Living. What do you think he was doing?' Crewlaw said as he threw himself back behind the wheel, then popped the door open and strode off toward the motel office. The way his boots crunched and slipped through the loose gravel reminded me of something female, but I couldn't quite put my finger on it. His anger was male, though. He seemed angry at everything these days. Maybe it was the death of his dad. I don't know.

I followed him as he pushed through the rusty screen door of the office into a little alcove/lobby and slapped the silver bell on the counter. It was one of those lobbies that look like the owners live in it day and night. A roll-away couch, with a plaid sleeping bag unzipped and spread across it like a blanket. Empty Winchell's doughnut boxes laying around. A caged blue parakeet smashing its beak into a tiny mirror and screaming on the same note. Some kind of miniature mongrel started yapping its brains out from a back room, then came charging down the hallway at us. Crewlaw stomped his foot at the dog and made like he was going to kick its head in, which caused the dog to flatten out on the floor, squealing. A short, dumpy woman came shuffling down the hallway wearing an orange muumuu and green go-aheads. She had her chin stuck in her neck and breathed like she was dying of emphysema. She called the dog's name in a sickening commiserating way that caused Crewlaw to grind his teeth when he spoke to her. 'My name's Crewlaw. I'm the son of the man who burned up here last week, and we were just wondering if we could see the bed. The mattress.'

'Yer name's what?'

'Crewlaw.'

'What kinda name's that?'

'Could we see the bed?'

'What bed?'

'The bed he burned up in.'

'We don't have no bed.'

'He was in room number six. He burned up in there. In bed. Mattress exploded.'

'Oh, that bed!' she said.

'Yeah, *that* bed. Could we see it? My friend doesn't believe me.'

'I believe you,' I said, wanting to turn tail and get the hell out of there.

'It's all burnt up,' she said.

'I know that. Could we see it, though?'

'What do you wanna see a burnt bed for? It's all waterlogged, too, from the fire hose. Lotsa damage in that room. Water damage. Smoke damage. Who's gonna pay for all that damage?'

'Not me,' Crewlaw said. 'That's for sure.'

'Then who? You're his son, right?'

'Yeah, right.'

'What'd you say your name was?'

'Crewlaw.'

'That's the one. Same name. I'd remember a name like that. What kinda name is that anyway?'

'Lithuanian.'

'Where's that?'

'Never mind. Could we see the bed or not?'

'It's thrown out.'

'Where'd you throw it out to?'

'Out back. It's leaning up against the building.'

'Okay if we go back there and take a look at it?'

'What're you gonna do with it?'

'We're not gonna do anything with it. I just wanna see it.'

'There isn't money in there or somethin', is there? If there's money in that mattress, you owe me some of it.'

'I don't owe you shit,' Crewlaw said, and turned back toward the door.

'You've got no call to come marching in here and foul-mouth me, buster! I don't care where you're from! I've got a good mind to call the highway patrol!'

'Kiss my white ass!' Crewlaw said as he slapped the screen door on her and crunched his way back into the parking lot. The dumpy woman's voice rose an octave from inside the lobby, and her small dog suddenly found his courage and started yapping in concert.

'I'm callin' the cops right now! You hear me! You think you can stroll in here in broad daylight and start insulting me to my face! Goddamn trash! No wonder yer dad burned up!'

We sprinted around to the back of the building and leaped a short black iron gate. Garbage cans lined the wall, capped with sun-bleached cat dishes caked with dried-up milk and tuna fish. Flies were having a heyday. 'There it is! Look at that! See?' Crewlaw's voice was full of vindication. The death mattress was standing on its end, leaning against a porch railing with a giant black hole burned clear through to daylight. It looked like a bomb had dropped on it. Crewlaw pulled it away from the railing and stuck his whole arm through the hole so his hand came out the other side. He opened and closed his fist, grabbing at air. The bluish-green pachuko cross tattooed between his thumb and first finger stretched and balled up with the action of his fist. I remembered the day Crewlaw had carved that cross in his hand with a penknife during geometry class. He kept poking the skin till it bled, then poured ink from a cartridge pen into the wound until it took hold. 'Burnt clear through. See that? That's what a cigar can do. Now maybe you can picture it.'

'We oughta get outa here, Crewlaw. She's gonna call the highway patrol.'

'You think the highway patrol is gonna come all the way out here because somebody called her names? They're not gonna do that.'

'I don't wanna get popped again in Azusa. If I get popped here again, I'm fucked.'

'You're not carrying nothin', are you?'

'No,' I said, 'but I don't wanna take any chances.'

'All right, grab ahold of this thing. Come on.'

'What're we doing?' I said.

'I'm taking it with me.'

'What for?'

'I just wanna take it with me. Now grab ahold!'

We walked the burned mattress out to the parking lot and threw it up on the roof of Crewlaw's car. He had some old bailing wire from the racetrack in the back seat, and we used that to strap the mattress down with. The miniature mongrel was still wailing away in the background, but there was no sign of the manager. Crewlaw's eyes snapped toward the office as he cinched down on the rusty wire. 'I'd shoot that sonofabitch if it was mine. Put it out of its misery.'

We took off with the mattress flopping on the roof and headed west past the Irwindale rock quarry, following the old Baseline Road through lemon groves and vineyards. The honeyed smell of lemon blossoms seemed confusing right then. The strange fear I was carrying didn't seem to mix with surrounding nature: a mockingbird in full raucous song; the pulsing mist of irrigated rain. The loud headers on the flathead Merc rumbled down through the floorboards, out into the immaculate aisles of lemon trees and oranges. I had a definite sense of somehow being a passenger in an evil vehicle cruising through Paradise. I had no idea how I'd come to be there. A coyote ducked off between the trees and headed for a deep ditch: a beautiful red coyote with a big ruff. He turned toward us and stopped a second, taking in the chopped and channeled Mercury with a burnt mattress flapping on the roof, then slipped away between the smudge pots and rain birds.

We turned off at Fish Canyon and drove up a gravel washboard road toward the Flood Control Aqueduct – a huge concrete serpent that swooped down from the San Gabriels and made its way to the desert. I'd never seen more than a trickle of water in it. The only flood I'd ever seen was in pictures of Alabama. I'd heard the main function of the aqueduct these days was as a dumping ground for murder victims from L.A., but I never saw a body in it either. Crewlaw pulled the Merc up right at the edge of the wide concrete canyon and jumped out. He paced a little up and down the edge of the aqueduct, staring out across the manzanita and yucca brush, then lit a Lucky Strike and turned back to me. 'Let's get this thing done,' he said, and went straight to the mattress and started unwinding the wire, as his cigarette bopped up and down between his lips. I helped him without asking what he had in mind.

We slid the mattress off the car roof and sent it flying end over end down the steep embankment. Maybe fifty feet it kicked and lurched, until it hit bottom and came to rest by a busted-up old washing machine – the kind with rollers on the top and a crank handle for squeezing the water out of clothes. Crewlaw stood there at the edge, staring down at it for a while as though making sure it had completely stopped moving. As though it might still have some life left in it. He flicked his Lucky Strike down the wall, then went straight to the trunk of his car and hauled out an orange gas can with a silver spout. He suddenly sprinted for the edge of the aqueduct and took a leap, disappearing like a suicide out a window. I followed him over the side and saw him galloping down the concrete face toward the mattress, with the gas can held high above his head. When we finally hit the flat bottom, both of us stopped and just stared at the mattress, panting for breath. The bottom smelled of dead fish and green algae.

Crewlaw poured all the gas on the mattress in little careful splashes, then threw the empty can in for good measure. 'Come on now, back away from it, 'cause this sucker's gonna blow,' he said, and tugged on my elbow. We walked off a ways, and he picked up a smooth, flat rock the color of cork. He took out his last three Lucky Strikes and dropped the rock into the empty wrapper, then crumpled it up good and tight. He set fire to the cellophane with his Zippo and waited until the flame turned from blue to orange, then tossed the burning rock with a little overhand flip like I'd seen him use on the basketball court. It looked like a faraway comet on its arc across the horizon, before it plunged into the mattress without a sound. There was a moment when nothing happened. We both thought it had gone out. No flame. Nothing. It almost whispered, then it took hold suddenly like a blast of desert wind, and the whole aqueduct lit up. 'Now he's *all* the way gone,' Crewlaw said as he stared at the column of swirling black smoke pouring out the hole in the mattress. 'Some people have to burn up twice, I guess.' The sun was just going down behind the concrete towers of the gravel refineries, with their tiny blue warning lights already blinking, and the black yucca standing silent along the ridge.

We drove out to spend the night at his aunt Mellie's in Cucamonga. She lived on the edge of an old abandoned vineyard, in one of those little clapboard box houses, originally thrown up for Mexican migrant workers. The wine business had moved way north. We passed the Blue Sky drive-in, where *Jailhouse Rock* was playing. We could see Elvis, huge against the dark purple mountains, singing silently and pumping his famous hips. I wondered what kind of jail he was in, where they allowed you to sing and dance like that, with a backup band, but I didn't mention it to Crewlaw. He never admitted to it, but Crewlaw had been trying hard to imitate Elvis's greaser duck-butt hairdo with the rainspout over the forehead. He used piles of Dixie Peach and Butchwax, but it never quite came together for him. It fell down too far over his eyes, giving him a sullen, dangerous look that cost him a lot of jobs. In fact, if it hadn't been for my personal recommendation, he probably would've never gotten hired onto the backstretch at Santa Anita. The management didn't like 'fair-ground trash,' and that's what Crewlaw's hairdo reminded them of. Trainers were always pretending to be clean-cut, wearing those dumb little tweed caps and spaghetti-string ties with a gold horseshoe clip. They had to maintain that pretense even though everyone knew they'd come up through the slop, just like us. Probably worse than us.

Crewlaw's aunt Mellie was half in the bag as always and never even got up from her sofa when she heard us coming. We just let ourselves in and headed straight for the kitchen. She called out to us from the front room, where she was watching *The Lone Ranger*. 'Don't you characters drink any a that beer in there! That beer's gotta last me two days!' Crewlaw gave me the eye and silently pried open the icebox, lifting out a bottle without so much as a tinkle. Aunt Mellie kept up her harangue from the sofa. 'Every now and then you might just give a thought to the other person, ya know! Wouldn't hurt. Wouldn't kill you a bit to be a little thoughtful!' We eased open the cap and sat at the Formica table, sliding the bottle between us and miming reactions to his aunt's little sermon. We had to plug our noses now and then to keep from bursting out loud and spitting beer all over the linoleum. 'Same problem with yer old man! That musta been where you picked it up. Same lack of considera- tion. Never had a thought for the other person. Not one notion.' We nodded in solemn agreement as the *William Tell* Overture played through the background to ricocheted gunshots, 'Kemo sabe,' and 'Hi-yo Silver, away!' Aunt Mellie was relentless: 'He just went his merry way, didn't he! Didn't give one hoot in hell about the consequences. Not to say that he ever did have any kind of future. Snakebit sonofabitch. Didn't surprise me one bit the way he passed. He deserved every inch of it. You think that's hard? I suppose you think I'm bein' hard, huh?' We shook our heads vehemently at each other and almost lost it. We doubled over in the spring-back chairs, clutching our bellies and praying for air. 'Well, nothin' was as hard as yer old man! The things he put yer mother through. It's a wonder she lived as long as she did. And all the damn excuses he had for his behavior. I never met a man with more excuses. Same as you! Excuses, excuses! What's yer big excuse tonight, Crewlaw! Answer me that!' Crewlaw straightened up in his chair and tried to get a grip on his spasms.

'Ma'm?'

'What's yer excuse tonight, I said! You heard me.'

'For what, ma'm?'

'Stumblin' in here, middle of the damn night, and stealin' my beer! I know what yer doin' in there.'

'It's not the middle of the night yet.'

'It's dark-thirty! Don't contradict me!'

'Yes, ma'm.'

'Stay outa that icebox, Crewlaw!'

'I'll get you a six-pack tomorrow, Aunt Mellie!'

'Tomorrow! You shoulda been born a damn Mexican with yer mañana disease. "Tomorrow"! That's the same song yer daddy sang. "Tomorrow, tomorrow"! Now he's got no tomorrow. How 'bout that. He's run flat out of tomorrows! How 'bout you?'

'How 'bout me, what, Aunt Mellie?' Crewlaw broke up completely this time and couldn't quite stifle the sounds. I leaned over and punched him in the knee, but it didn't help.

'You might think this is a big comedy, I suppose! All this agony and torture for the sake of a big laugh! Is that how you see it?'

'No, ma'm!'

'You'll be laughin' out the other side of yer damn head in about ten years time! Maybe sooner! Believe you me. Things happen before you even know it.'

'Yes, ma'm!'

'Layin' up in some Christ-less flophouse just like yer old man. Staring at the cracks in the plaster. Wondering what ever became of yer life. See how much of a comedy it is then, big shot!' She went silent after that, but *The Lone Ranger* continued, then was broken by a frantic Cal Worthington Dodge commercial. We tiptoed over to the open doorway and peeked in at her, laying on her threadbare sofa. Her back was to us. She had on a blue bandanna and a pink fuzzy sweater with the sleeves pulled up to her elbows. A faded Mexican blanket covered her from the waist down. One arm hung almost to the floor, with an L & M burning a long gray ash. She didn't move. Her fingers were stained yellow, with huge knuckles, like a man's. She wore a silver thunderbird ring set with a turquoise. The cigarette smoke snaked around the ring and up her arm to the pink sweater.

She never moved. She spoke without turning around to us. Her voice was different now. Deeper. Almost male. 'I know yer watching me,' she said. 'Go ahead and watch. You won't see nothin'.'

3/5/89 (LOS ANGELES)

A Small
Circle of
Friends

In the mid-fifties my parents had a small circle of friends. By 1961 they'd all disappeared. Later, I found out this was partly due to my father's drinking and his ensuing temper tantrums. The kind of temper tantrums where you thought his head might explode. Sometime around 1957 there was a barbecue at our place, where all these friends of theirs convened. There was Ted Maysley, a tall, slender man with a steel-gray crew cut that stood up high on his head like an inverted shoe brush. He was only in his forties but solid gray. He played piano and sang Fats Waller tunes and always wore a suit and tie. The suits were always gray to match his crew cut. Much later, I found out Ted had hanged himself from his garage rafter because he'd discovered he was gay. There was Lance Torrace and his wife, Louise. Louise I found very sexy, and they had an equally sexy daughter, named Liza, about my age; about thirteen. Me and Liza used to sneak out by the sheep pens and fool around. She was very exciting to fool around with, because she made noises like Jayne Mansfield used to make in her movies with Mickey Hargitay. Liza's mother, Louise, had amazing hips. They were powerful, and she always had them cinched up into slinky midcalf skirts, where you could see her garter buttons bulging out. Much later, I found out Louise had thrown herself off a two-story veranda and landed facedown on their Spanish-tile patio and snapped her neck. Lance, her husband, a former football coach, slowly went mad over the next decade and lost his entire shoe business. There were Lou and Doris Parnell, who liked cards and played the horses a lot. You could always tell what kind of luck they were having by the style of car they drove. If they were winning, it would be a Thunderbird. When they lost, it became a Plymouth. There was an Italian-looking man named Phil, who was the object of a lot of controversy in our house. My father repeatedly accused my mother of having an affair with him, but I never saw him take the accusation directly to Phil. Instead, my father would periodically destroy different rooms in the house: always late at night, after me and my sisters were supposed to be asleep. He always contained his violence within one room, and in the morning, there was no mistaking which room it was. His favorite was the kitchen.

This particular barbecue in 1957 seemed to be getting off the ground pretty well. It was a bright afternoon, and the apricots were just ripening on the trees. A gentle wind from the San Joaquin drew the smell of hamburgers, chicken, and orange blossoms across the yard and out into the avocado orchard. Liza was throwing a rubber bone for our dog and chasing him hysterically. She kept working her way down toward the sheep pens and giving me little darting looks back over her shoulder. I pretended not to notice. Arturo, a Mexican friend my father had hired to do some yardwork, was cutting cooch grass with a Toro power mower. He was a very quiet-faced man, who wore a floppy straw hat and huaraches with soles made from old tire treads. He told me he'd been in trouble down in Chihuahua City with some very bad men and had been forced to leave Mexico. He never would tell me the details, but he said it involved a woman. He used to carve serpent designs into little pruned branches of fruitwood and give them to me. I collected all of them in a drawer with my jackknives.

The small circle of friends was having a great time. My mother's high-pitched genuine laughter rang out over the rest of the voices, signaling to me that she'd already had a couple. Everybody was drinking and clinking and talking at once. Even my father seemed temporarily happy, poking at the sizzling flesh with a long fork and sipping his beer. Ted was singing: 'You're not the only wrinkle on the prune. You're not the only apple on the tree. Nevertheless, I confess – positively, positively – you're the only one for me.' Doing his best Waller imitation, punctuating the end of each verse with a lusty 'Yeah!' while Phil added little improvised vocal trombone phrases to the chorus. He'd close his eyes, and his lips would kind of flap up and down and buzz when he did this. He accompanied his buzzing lips with slide trombone gestures, using the hand he held his drink with. His drink would splash a little into Ted's lap with each slide, but Ted didn't seem to notice. Phil never opened his eyes to see what a mess he was making. He was too far gone. Lance, Louise, Lou, Doris, and my mother were in fits over something they'd just remembered from their college days. Something a good twenty years before, about a homecoming queen. My mother must have remembered it best, because she was laughing loudest. These were the only occasions I can remember my parents laughing at the same time in the same place: these little get-togethers of theirs.

What happened next was that Liza came running up to the house without the rubber bone, our dog chasing her like he thought she was still playing with him, but she wasn't. She was crying. She ran straight to her mother and grabbed hold of her waist and buried her head in Louise's skintight white skirt. Everyone stopped talking and laughing and drinking except Ted and Phil, who were on the last verse of 'Honeysuckle Rose.' Pretty soon, even they stopped, and they took their drinks out on the patio to see why the party mood had suddenly shifted gears. Everyone split up into pairs, and hardly anyone spoke. The ones who did speak sort of whispered to each other, stared at the ground, and slowly shook their heads. Louise and Liza went inside the house with my mother who kept patting Liza softly on the shoulder and stroking her head. Lance went up to my father and said right to his face: 'I told you about hiring Mexicans, didn't I?' then he went straight into the house and left my father standing there. My father took his Bar-B-Q apron off and set down the long fork beside the grill. He stared into the glowing briquettes, and his whole face emptied out. There was no anger in it, just a long anguish that seemed to return to him as though he knew these brief lapses into happiness were only temporary masks to his real fate. Ted patted my father on the back, but my father never looked at him or acknowledged the kind gesture. He just walked off slowly and headed for the sheep pens. He walked like he didn't want to go down there; like he was following orders from somebody else's conscience. I followed him but not close enough to piss him off. His mind was somewhere else anyway, and he never even noticed me. Our dog was dancing around me in stupid circles, his tail flashing back and forth; he grinned up at me, his tongue lolling out. He was happy and stupid like that all the time. No matter what happened.

I could see Arturo sitting in his old green Chevy pickup, with the Toro mower and his yard tools sticking out the back. He was sitting very still, without his hat and with both his leathery brown hands on the wheel, like he was expecting my father to come down there and give him a talking-to. His truck wasn't running. My father walked right up to the truck and sat down in the cab, next to Arturo. The door made a horrible cracking sound when he closed it. They didn't look at each other for a long time. They didn't speak. They just stared straight out the windshield at nothing. Arturo gripped the steering wheel as though they were driving, but the truck wasn't even running. For a second it looked as though they could be two men on a cross-country trip, but the truck wasn't moving. The sheep started bleating like they thought there was hay coming, and they lined the fence, poking their noses through the mesh. Our dog ran back and forth along the fenceline with his head low, snapping at lambs and barking his head off. My father and Arturo just stared out the dusty windshield. Then my father said something in Spanish to Arturo, without turning his head to him, and Arturo cranked the ignition, and they drove off together, very slowly. I watched the green truck go down the hill, past the eucalyptus, and disappear, with the mower and tools bouncing in the bed.

When I got back to the house, everyone was leaving except Lance, Louise, and Liza. My mother was talking quietly with Lance in the kitchen at the red table. Her voice was full of apology. Lance was smoking and staring at the linoleum. Louise and Liza had gone into my parents' bedroom and shut the door. I could hear Louise's voice even through the door: 'I've told you a dozen times not to wear that bra! You're too young to be wearing a bra like that!' I said good-bye to Ted and shook his hand. I remember thinking he was a gentleman. There was something very kind about his eyes. That was the last time I saw him alive, and if I'd known that at the time, I'd have said something to him about his kindness. How unusual it was. Lou and Doris were waving to me from their Plymouth as they backed out the driveway. They seemed happily drunk and not caught up in the recent circumstances. I waved back. I saw Phil in the front yard, circling an orange tree with a drink in his hand and a cigarette. He kept kicking at the grass and staring down at his brogans, then rubbing the tips of them on the back of his calves. He'd look back at the house, then keep circling and swirling his glass. I could hear his ice tinkling. Ted gave two little beeps on his horn as he drove off, and Phil raised his glass to him, but he didn't look up. He just kept circling the orange tree and kicking at the lawn. White smoke was drifting across the yard as the barbecue petered out.

After a while my mother came outside with Lance, Louise, and Liza. Liza's face was red and streaky-looking, but she wasn't crying now. She gave a little peek at me, then ducked behind her mother's waist. All I could see was one eye, which seemed full of guilt. My mother walked them all over to their car, with her arms crossed on her chest and her head down. She kissed Liza on the cheek and closed the door softly when Liza got in. She waved good-bye to them as they drove off and kept right on waving when they were out of sight, as though they were going far away. Phil stopped circling the orange tree and raised his glass to my mother when she turned back toward the house. She stopped and stared at him. She didn't smile. Then she turned toward me and stared as if she'd suddenly lost track of things. I went into the house and watched them from behind the curtains at the kitchen window. I watched her cross the lawn toward Phil, in her high heels. Phil was smiling and smoking, like he thought he was in the movies.

His chest blew up. He cocked one hip and flicked his cigarette, then took a deep drag. Just as my mother reached him, I saw Arturo's green truck pulling up the hill. My mother saw it too, and she turned abruptly and walked straight back toward the house, trying to look as though that's where she'd been heading all along. Phil called out to her, but she never looked back at him. She kept walking, shaking her head, and crossed her arms tight on her chest, as if she was warding off some cold chill. Phil stomped his cigarette in the grass and took a slug from his drink. Arturo's truck stopped on the road in front of the yard, and my father stepped out. He stood there on the road, staring through the oleander bushes at Phil, as Arturo drove off.

My mother came into the kitchen, patting her chest and breathing fast, blowing each breath out on the exhale. She told me to get away from the window, and when I asked her why, she said, 'Just do it!' She went straight to the bedroom and shut the door hard behind her. I could hear her throw her high heels at the wall, and then it was quiet.

I stayed at the kitchen window and watched my father walk, stooped over, through the tall hedge bushes toward Phil, rather than take the long way around up the driveway. Phil turned toward my father and raised what was left in his glass. Phil smiled and reached for his pack of cigarettes. My father hit Phil so hard the glass exploded in Phil's face. Ice went flying into the orange tree. When Phil put his hands up to protect his eyes, my father grabbed Phil by the hair and smashed his face down into his raised knee. He did this over and over again. I could hear Phil's nose split, even from that far away, but Phil never made a sound. Then he slumped down to the grass, and my father just left him there. He walked away and turned the rainbird sprinklers on and let them wash back and forth over Phil. A turquoise humming-bird darted in and out of the misty water spray.

That night I took all the little carved serpent sticks that Arturo had given me and lined them up on my bed. I kept rearranging them in different designs as I listened to my father destroy another room.

Next morning, I left town for good. I took all my jack-knives and serpent sticks with me.

4/4/89 (LOS ANGELES)

Fear
of the
Fiddle

Fall of 1963, I took a job with the Burns Detective Agency to guard coal barges on the East River. It was my very first job in New York City. I had no idea why coal barges on the East River might be in jeopardy, but I took the job gladly, since the day before I'd had to resort to selling a pint of blood on Times Square in order to buy a cheeseburger. I reported to the Burns office in midtown, feeling slightly light-headed but eager to get started. They outfitted me with a khaki uniform, a nightstick, a punch-out clock in a black leather holster that hung from the shoulder, and a bright silver badge. My hours were 10:00 p.m. until dawn. I sat on a brown metal fold-out chair in a little wooden guard booth about the size of an outhouse. There was just enough room in there for a small electric heater, which clanked and blasted my feet with hot air but didn't keep any of the rest of me warm. Every fifteen minutes I was supposed to make my rounds of the docks, stopping at designated steel posts with little boxes mounted on them containing keys. This was their way of keeping tabs on me. I'd fit each key into a slot in my punch-out clock and turn it, causing a notch on a paper disk, which I'd drop in a box at the end of the night. Then I'd hike home to Avenue C and Tenth Street, into the rising sun.

Dawn was the best time to walk the streets of New York; especially in a khaki uniform with a nightstick. I seemed like the only one out there except for the whine of garbage trucks and the men bundled up against the cold in their corner newsstands. I felt an affinity with these men; all of us working in outhouse-size boxes with little clacking electric heaters. The smokestacks of Con Ed spewed out long columns of white fume into the morning light. Lone junkies staggered out of all-night doughnut shops, with haunted, haggard eyes. I was a long way from Duarte, but it felt good to have gone through the whole night with no sleep and be getting paid for it.

It was this proposition of no sleep that led me into an area of experimentation. I was introduced to a substance called crystal methedrine by an Appalachian fiddle player named Ansel Cartwright, who I'd met on the Lower East Side. His method of intake was to mix the bitter powder with straight Coca-Cola and belt the whole thing down. Our personal record for no sleep was five consecutive days. Ansel was a walking encyclopedia of early American folk and mountain music but laid no claims to being a purist. 'Far as I'm concerned, "Blueberry Hill" is folk music. Same for Little Richard.' His fiddle was lacquered candy-apple green, with a pin-striped spiderweb painted on the back in black. The bright-green beast was electrified but could be unplugged and played acoustic, as the situation demanded. Ansel liked to accompany me on my new detective job on the docks. He liked the peacefulness of the setting. The oily purple water gently lapping the prows of the barges. The distant moan of tugboats and tankers signaling one another through the harbor. The glittering lights of Manhattan, invoking more the vision of a village than a major metropolis. We'd squeeze into the tiny guardhouse on chilly nights, with our king-size bottle of laced Coca-Cola tucked into a corner next to the heater. Ansel had to play his fiddle standing up, and the door had to be cracked open to allow room for his bowing elbow hacksawing out into the night air. A few hits on our bottle of Coke, and we were both impervious to cold and time. The only other instrument that would fit in there was a pair of nickel-plated soup spoons that I'd picked up in a pawnshop. I played those spoons off my knees and hands, and we'd improvise through 'I'm Goin' Fishin'' for fifteen-minute intervals until it was time for me to punch the stupid clock again. Sometimes Ansel would just keep right on playing and follow me out there with his fiddle as I patrolled the dock. He'd weave and bob in front of a full moon, bowing furiously until the horsehair bow started to come unraveled in long wispy strands. He'd keep right on playing and follow me back to the guardhouse, where I'd pick up, the spoons again and continue through another fifteen-minute session, until our arms seized up. Then we'd sit there and sip on our bottle and talk about things like the ancient fear of the fiddle. According to Ansel, it seems the early American colonists had inherited certain occult superstitions from the European religious fanatics of the Middle Ages. One of these was the belief that the fiddle was an instrument of the Devil himself. It was an absolutely forbidden instrument throughout colonial America. No one was even allowed to own a fiddle, much less play one. Nevertheless covert fiddle societies began to spring up. They would gather deep in the woods under cover of darkness and hang their fiddles in oak trees, leaving them overnight under the full moon in the belief that the Devil would visit the instrument and inhabit the wood with his spirit. Other factions feared this possession by the Devil and carved grotesque faces into the necks of their fiddles to ward off any visitation. Fiddle contests sprang out of these early clandestine meetings, similar to those found on the Mississippi Delta between guitar players two hundred years later. At the heart of these contests was the persistent belief in the Devil's influence over the music. If a fiddler demonstrated a particular flair for improvisation and seemed to drift off into a world of his own, this was a sure sign of his conspiring with the Dark Forces. Ansel himself admitted to being slightly superstitious. He burned Puerto Rican votive candles inside our little guardhouse. The sweet smell was almost enough to gag you. Each candle had a different color and odor, corresponding to its application. Green was supposed to attract money and had a stinging peppermint smell. Red was for good luck in love and smelled like spoiled cherries. White was for health and smelled like vanilla. By the end of the night, neither one of us had any desire for breakfast. Another thing Ansel had was a John the Conquerroot. I'd never seen one before, but I'd heard about them in songs. He carried it in a little leather satchel tied to his belt. It looked like a dried-up lime with brown warts all over it. He said he'd swapped it for a 1948 Gibson flattop, which was worth a whole lot of money, even in those days. The really tough part about Ansel's visits to my little guardhouse was his practice of wearing garlic all over his person. He said he used it to ward off demons. He carried cloves of it in every pocket and even crushed some up in his boots so that it would enter through the soles of his feet. In a four-by-four-foot box with smelly candle smoke, garlic, and a beat-up electric heater whirring away, things were getting a little close.

After the hookup with Ansel I only lasted about a week more on the Burns job. One night we got so absorbed in an extended version of 'Soldier's Joy' that I completely forgot my rounds with the punch-out clock. Next day I was history with the agency. They wanted the uniform back, the cap, the nightstick, the clock, and, of course, the badge. They laid heavy emphasis on the return of the badge. I returned everything but the clock, which I threw in the East River. Ansel played a dirge called 'Lowlands' as we watched it slowly sink between the barges.

When I got back to Avenue C, there was a letter waiting for me from the U.S. Government. Vietnam was gearing up.

5/16/89 (SCOTTSVILLE, VIRGINIA)

Dignity

I always meant to thank you for saving me from that
mattress on the floor of Eighth Street. It was great of you. I
don't exactly know how everything got so run-down and
messy; my life included. I never told you, but just before
we'd met, I'd finally gotten over an embarrassing disease
that, to this day, I still don't know how I contracted. A
couple of airline stewardesses had dropped in, weeks before,
and one of them had spent some time in Brazil. I think it
must have been her I caught it from. In any case, at that
time, I was working as a busboy at the Hickory House
uptown, where they have the famous horseshoe piano bar. (I
think I told you this.) I was in charge of the big round table
at the back, which was always reserved for Duke Ellington
and his family. I'll never forget him sitting there in his silver
suits and ties, surrounded by his wife and daughters. He was
a truly regal man if ever I saw one. There was such a great,
natural dignity about him and a kindness that seemed to

spread directly through his children. I remember watching his long, ringed fingers breaking bread, as I poured their ice water and placed the butter down. 'Those are the fingers that play "Satin Doll"! Those very same fingers!' I said to myself. I was in such excruciating pain then, between my legs, that I had to walk bowlegged so nothing would rub. It was a real fancy steak house, and I tried to be as subtle as possible about my walk so the headwaiter wouldn't notice and fire me on the spot. But I can tell you, the pain was unbelievable.

Somehow, the presence of 'Sir Duke' made everything go away for a while, and I dreamed of one day becoming a benevolent patriarch with a magnificent wife and children who never scream.

Anyhow, thanks for the great croissants with marmalade and the view of Spanish Harlem.

Yours.

5/4/95 (SCOTTSVILLE, VIRGINIA)

More
Urgent
Emergencies

She was cutting a huge slice of watermelon on the kitchen counter with one of those serrated stainless-steel bread knives with the wavy blades. She'd just come in from working in the garden, and it must've been ninety-nine degrees out there. It had stayed in the nineties for days now.

I came up behind her and wrapped my arms around her waist, licking the sweat off the back of her neck. She tilted her head back next to mine and kept sawing the knife down through the red flesh of the watermelon, and when it reached the rind she gave an extra little hard press with one hand on the handle and the other on the tip. At first I didn't even feel it. It just felt like a dull electric shock, like the kind you get when you slide off a wool couch and touch a doorknob. Blood went everywhere, and neither of us knew where it was coming from. It was spraying all over the kitchen. She turned and faced me. There were little droplets of blood all over her, like someone had shaken a wet paintbrush at her. 'What's wrong?' she said, and I had no idea either until I looked down and saw the last joint of my little finger lying there by the watermelon, all by itself. I held my left hand up, and the blood was pumping onto her gardening dress.

She drove me down to the emergency room, while I kept my left hand vertical, wrapped in ice cubes with a dish towel. I had the tip of my little finger bound up in a piece of Kleenex and stuffed into my right pocket. Hot wind blew through the windows, and some crows pulling on the intestine of a dead rabbit waited until the last second to fly out of the way of our car.

We walked through the electric doors of the hospital, the kind that suddenly bolt back away from you, clearing the space for a possible stretcher and a swarm of paramedics. There were several emergencies ahead of us that day: a bad motorcycle wreck, a shotgun accident, and a stabbing. A group of young Chicanos was huddled in a corner, weeping and holding one another in quiet grief.

We filled out all the necessary forms, with her doing most of the writing since I kept bleeding all over the paperwork. A nurse with a superprofessional air about her had a look at my finger and cleaned it up with Betadine and peroxide, which turned my entire hand a kind of leathery orange color. It reminded me of the stains I used to get from the first baseball glove of the season, a J. C. Higgins. With my good hand, I pulled out the severed tip of my little finger and unwrapped it from the Kleenex with my teeth. The serious nurse took the piece of my finger, dropped it into a clear plastic Ziploc bag, and put it on ice. She did this like a cop would handle an item of evidence at a crime scene.

We waited in the waiting room, watching people thumb through colorful magazines on golf and real estate and animal husbandry. Two women in their seventies were consoling each other about a man they must have both been related to: 'I knew it was coming, I just didn't think it would be on us so soon.'

'I know, Helen, but you've got to shore yourself up now. For his sake. You've got to just put on a brave face.'

'I'm not prepared, Doreen. I thought I would be, but I'm just not ready for this. He seemed so healthy.' Helen broke down sobbing into Doreen's shoulder, and Doreen patted her forehead with a little blue handkerchief.

A nurse came out into the waiting room, calling the name of a Spanish couple. The couple jumped to attention, the man snatching his baseball cap off his head and holding the brim with both hands over his turquoise belt buckle. The woman held her purse in the same way that he held his cap, and they both marched off, following the nurse. By their stoic Indian faces you could tell it was their child at stake.

We kept waiting in the waiting room, and I put my good hand on her left knee and held it there while the other hand throbbed with blood. Her knee felt cool and silky. She told me she was sorry and kissed my ear. I told her it was just an accident and that it was great just to be sitting there with her, holding her perfect knee.

The doctor said it probably wasn't going to work – sewing the digit back onto my little finger. The risk of infection was very high. I asked him how come we had to wait so fucking long in the goddamn waiting room, allowing time for the tip of my finger to atrophy. He said it couldn't be helped. There were more urgent emergencies than mine. Lives were at stake. He put lives above fingers. I couldn't argue with him there. He told me he'd give it a shot, though, and attempt to rejoin the finger.

As he proceeded to thread the sutures, the doctor told us a little anecdote. He talked and sewed in a matter-of-fact way, without the slightest sense that he was trying to distract me from the pain. He said, 'The Plains Indians had a very interesting ritual applicable to fingers. They would sever a finger as a sign of mourning for the loss of a loved one. The little finger was equivalent to a child. The ring finger, a wife. The index finger, a parent, and so on. That's why if you look very closely at some of those old photographs of that tragic period when they were being interned in government camps, if you examine the hands of the very oldest members of a tribe, you'll notice that some of them have no fingers left at all on either hand. Just stubs.'

We drove back to the house and cleaned up all the blood in the kitchen. All the chrome appliances, the cupboards, the tile floor. As we worked, we told each other our impressions of the accident. They were basically the same. Neither of us could understand where the blood was coming from when all we were doing was kissing.

4/6/89 (LOS ANGELES)

*You I
Have No
Distance
From*

I can't remember what it was like before I met you. Was I
always like this? I remember myself lost. I know that for
sure. Wandering. Moving from one wild woman to the
next. Staying, sometimes, just long enough to understand
that their bewilderment was more pronounced than mine.
At least that's the way they put it across. But I can't
remember being this nervous before; this frazzled. I'd
watch them from a distance: taking stoned sponge baths in
their sinks; shaving black hash balls with razor blades;
moving like slow-motion queens. Then they'd change into
backyard girls from long ago, giggling and tucking their
long legs up under themselves: the way they'd plunk down
on their soft heels and then toss their hair like horses switch
their tails.

But you I have no distance from. Every move you make
feels like I'm traveling in your skin; every glance you take
out the window, as though you were completely alone and

dreaming in some other time. It does no good to wave my arms. Now everything's reversed.

5/15/95 (SCOTTSVILLE, VIRGINIA)

Thin Skin

This was the third straight time that J.D. had been popped for shoplifting at Wal-Mart. The assistant manager there was a gung-ho trainee kid who had developed a real grudge against J.D. over the months and got very excited about the arrest, certain that this would mean his promotion to manager itself. What they caught J.D. with was a roll of Kodachrome and an electric toothbrush. That was it.

I went bail for him, and we took a long walk down by the freeway, with J.D. talking; very down on himself, listing his long string of failures. He called himself the 'Professional Failure' and went clear back to his days as a veterinary assistant when he got fired for photographing an Airedale fucking a dachshund after closing time. His main arena of failure, though, the one he liked to harp on most, was women. Dozens of women. According to J.D., it was women in general who had driven him to this life of petty crime and one in particular, a girl named Lola, who was responsible for his current state of crisis. He wanted to run to her now and get all worked up about his latest arrest; tell her if she only knew how much he loved her he wouldn't be in the shape he was in, and have a real knock-down passionate confrontation like that. I got him calm and persuaded him not to go to Lola but to just keep on walking.

We walked clear to San Rafael that night, following the trail of the frontage roads and the taillights of commuter traffic. It was January something and cold as shit, and J.D. hated cold with a passion. His skin would start shedding like a snake every winter about this time, and he'd have to wear lots of Nivea Creme and double layers of army-surplus long underwear, causing him to walk wide and stiff-legged. Why girls ever fell for him I never could figure out, but he was miraculous at a bar. He'd have them coming over to his table in giggling pairs, introducing themselves; buying him whiskey sours; scribbling their phone numbers on cocktail napkins, then rushing off to the bathroom and reemerging in full model makeup. I asked one of these girls once what she found so attractive about J.D., and she told me it was his terrific sense of humor: something he'd lost track of this particular night.

We were carrying our trusty silver flasks, filled with a Wild Turkey/Drambuie mix, and J.D. had a couple of really badly rolled joints on him: the kind where the seeds bulge out of the paper, causing them to pop and hiss like Chinese firecrackers every time you take a hit. It was god-awful pot, which left green stripes on your lower lip and smelled rank and swampy. We got high enough to forget about the cold, though, and started singing 'The Blue Ridge Mountains of Virginia' in harmony and doing that little skip-and-stroll Laurel and Hardy dance step from their movie about the French Foreign Legion. The freeway roared beside us. The moon was one of those upside-down crescent jobs like they have on the Turkish flag. Blue TV light flashed from the condominiums, and straight people all over were having their supper.

It was right in the middle of the second verse of the Laurel and Hardy tune that J.D. came unraveled. It was so dramatic I thought he was kidding at first. He hit the ground hard with both knees, clutching at his chest and breathing like he'd been hit in the gut with a baseball bat. His teeth were clacking and he rolled his eyes back, blinking up at the skinny moon. A chain-link guard fence separated us from the freeway, and J.D. clawed onto it and tried to haul himself up to his feet. Cars were pouring past us, maybe five feet away, blasting pockets of wind into our faces. I grabbed hold of his shoulders and tried to get out of him which part of his body was failing: 'Is it your heart, J.D.? Are you having one of those middle-aged heart attacks, or what?' He just kept panting and weaving his head like he wanted to speak, but only one word came out of him: 'LOLA!' I told him to forget about her. Forget about Lola altogether. Get her out of his head; she wasn't going to save him now. He turned to me with blind terror in his eyes, as though I'd robbed him of his last idea on earth. He screamed her name and tore at his chest. He grabbed higher on the fence and started to climb, punching the toes of his janitor shoes into the diamond-shaped spaces, trying to get a foothold and slipping, then churning his legs and clawing his way slowly to the top. Every time I'd grab his leg he'd try to kick me in the face, yelling things like: 'SHE IS MY HEART! SHE IS MY ONLY HEART!' Cars were beginning to notice us now, honking wildly, blinking their lights, and swerving out of the lane to avoid us. We both straddled the top pipe of the chain link, looking down on an eight-lane raging river of traffic. J.D. was screaming at the traffic now, while I tried to keep him from falling: 'SHE IS MY WIND! SHE IS THE

VERY BREATH I BREATHE!' Truck drivers were giving us the finger and pointing spotlights at us as they blasted their air horns. It must have been the suction from the traffic below that caused J.D. to lose his balance. He pitched over backward, catching his pant leg on the top wire. He just hung there, upside down, for a while, flailing his arms and screaming her name like a chant. It was the most pathetic thing I'd ever seen. I finally got his leg cut loose with my Ka-Bar jackknife, and he flopped down to the long wet grass below and just lay there, spread-eagled like a dead man, for the longest time.

After I got him collected again, he refused to return to his rented room that night. He lived in a converted garage off Olive in Corte Madera, and he said the place harbored too many ghosts for him. I checked him into a little bungalow motel called El Sueño, right off the 101 freeway. The motel manager apologized for the phones being out of order, but when we got into the room there was no phone at all. All the lightbulbs were missing, so we had to use the light of the TV, keeping the sound turned off. I got a few more belts of the Wild Turkey mix into J.D., and he settled down enough to where I could at least put him to bed. He refused to take any of his clothes off, though, and he kept having convulsions of weeping and shivers. It was the kind of weeping you hear in the back alleys of Mexico City. Beyond anguish. My heart went out to him, but what could I do?

I asked him if he wanted to maybe try and get hold of this Lola of his, and he told me it wouldn't do any good. She was through with him forever. Then he got real sick, and I spent a long time cleaning it up, because there was only one skimpy little hand towel and a paper shower mat to work with. I opened up the sliding glass window to air the place out, and the sound of the freeway came rushing in. I went out on the little balcony and looked down at the traffic.

The cars were almost directly below me. For no good reason, I remembered a history book from the fifth grade called *El Camino Real*, with a scene pictured on the cover from the old Spanish days of early California: a sandal-footed, chubby priest in a brown robe leading a burro down a dirt road, shaded by feathery pepper trees. In the background was a golden mission, with three bells in the tower. The padre had a beatific smile on his moon face and looked like he knew where he was going, sent by God himself and the Spanish Crown.

I turned back into the room, and J.D. was having the shakes again: rolling in the bed, hugging himself, and yelling at me to close the fucking window. The cold air was killing him, he said. He said he could feel the cold clear through to his bones.

I sat with him all night, like you do with old relatives in the hospital, halfway hoping to find some escape. I didn't hold his hand or anything, but I listened to him, and what I heard was a long lostness that traveled way back inside him to the voice of a little boy. He sounded just like a kid of about eight or nine years old, and in that voice he told me things that I could barely make out. Just little glimpses of things that came into his mind. Places. People he remembered. Aunts and uncles whose names I'd never heard him speak before. A candy store in Hoboken. He was sweating and tossing, then he'd suddenly get very calm and lucid and come more into the present. His voice came back to the one I recognized as his own, and he'd talk about Lola and how they'd met at the Trailways bus station in Gilroy. The way they used to sit all day in Denny's, having coffee and talking. The way they were never apart. He told me she was born in the sixties and named after some girl in a Kinks tune. He said he was going to die without her. That's what he was doing now. Dying, he said. He knew he was dying.

Around 5:00 a.m. I wrote him a note explaining where I was going and when I'd be back, and I placed it in the center of his chest as he slept. The note kept slipping with his breathing, so I made a little slit in it with my knife and buttoned it to his shirt, just like the notes my uncle used to button on me before the first day of school.

I went looking for Lola and tracked her down through a return address I found on one of her letters in J.D.'s pocket. They were fabulous letters, full of passion and picturesque sex scenes. I read every one, without the least twinge of guilt or betrayal, and when I finished them all I understood very clearly how he could fall so completely under her spell. She had a voice in those letters that spoke directly to the blood of a middle-aged man.

I took the bus to Novato and picked up my Buick. It was one of those mornings when you can actually see the paradise side of northern California. You can see it right through all the human mess. Snowy egrets gliding across the marshlands. Hawks perched on fence posts, watching traffic. Holsteins grazing in the lush emerald grass. I wasn't really looking forward to this confrontation with Lola. I wasn't sure how she'd take it. She didn't know me from Adam, and according to J.D., she'd already made up her mind about him. What was I supposed to do?

I stood there on her front porch in one of those crummy little Vallejo suburbs left over from the fifties, and my whole body started to shake. I couldn't figure this out. Whether it was just the apprehension about talking to her or if it might have something to do with her letters. They were really incredible letters. I mean, no woman had ever written *me* letters like that. She'd gone into such detail about things, with complete tenderness.

She didn't answer the door like a regular person answers a door. There was no 'Who is it? What do you want?' kind of suspicion. She just appeared and stared at me through the screen door, with a plastic water glass full of red wine. She sat across from me on a couch with her legs tucked up and kept pushing her peach-colored bathrobe down between her thighs. She sipped on her wine and never offered me any. I hate wine anyway. She explained very softly, very simply, why she'd broken things off with J.D. 'He was a great seducer,' she said. 'And that's what women are always ready for – real seduction. We love that. To be coerced. The falling-in-love part. Trouble is, most men are no good at it. They lack imagination. That's what J.D. had. Imagination. He made himself into a big mystery. He really got me going. It took me months to figure him out. He'd been telling me all along that his main profession was as a private detective. He'd showed me his card and badge the very first time I ever met him; and he gave me no reason to think he was lying. He showed me his gun, his files of cases he was working on, his tape recorder and camera. He'd take me with him on surveillance assignments: watching houses from the car; following husbands who were cheating on wives; stuff like that. It was very exciting. We'd sit in his car for hours, watching a house, drinking beer, talking and smoking. Then we'd follow some poor guy, clear into the city sometimes. We'd check into the same hotel and get a room right next to his. We'd wiretap the wall and take pictures of the guy as he snuck his mistress in and out of the elevator. It was real thrilling. Better than being in a movie. I'd never been involved with a private detective before. It was a whole new life for me. We'd make love in the room, right next door to the unfaithful husband. We could hear him moaning and groaning as we made love in silence. We were absolutely silent in this, which was another thing that turned me on. We could hear the guy's girlfriend yelling out his name, but we never made a sound ourselves. And we never laughed at their outcries either. We never made fun of them behind their backs. J.D. had honor like that. He said, "Men lead pathetic lives," and then he'd kiss me like he wanted to prove he wasn't one of them – one of the pathetic.'

She turned her head away from me for a second and stared out the window. I couldn't tell if the memory of J.D. had called up some emotion in her or if she was just trying to find the thread of her failed romance. She had a great face. One of those on-the-level faces that cause you to sink down into yourself. I followed the line of her neck down to her collarbone, hoping she didn't turn back to face me for a while. She was definitely alone in this life. She had that feeling about her: like she'd accepted it. The opposite of J.D. I tried to carefully explain to her his condition – what he was going through without her. She turned to me and smiled. It was a kind smile, without the slightest hint of venom toward J.D. She said, 'He should have understood what I meant to him when we were together. Now it's too late. It wasn't the lying about his job so much that got me. It was the lying about himself. Pretending something. That's what got me. See, he took this surveillance thing way too far. The whole detective bit. Instead of leveling with me, he decided to take it to its ultimate moment. The big payoff. He drove me out to the house of the betrayed wife, and J.D. had the time schedules all figured out, so he knew the husband wasn't going to be there. Funny thing was, he probably would've made a great private detective in real life. He really had a knack for it. Anyhow, I stayed in the car and watched him as he went up to the front door and rang the bell. I watched the whole exchange between him and the wife, like a silent movie. I watched him show her the pictures we'd taken of her husband with his mistress. He kept looking back over his shoulder at me to see if I was paying attention to his procedure. Make sure I wasn't missing any of the details. I watched the wife break down and start weaving from side to side, pulling at the sleeves of her sweater and sobbing. She stared at the pictures and shook her head, then swung her face toward the sky with her hand on her mouth. J.D. kept looking back at me through all this as though searching for some sign of approval from me. I suddenly realized he was doing this all for my benefit. It was some kind of show. He was putting this woman through all this horrible misery just for me. I turned the ignition on and drove off in his car. He chased me for blocks, waving his arms and screaming like a fool. I lost him down by Sycamore and ditched the car. I just walked away from it. That was the last time I ever saw him. I remember him in the rearview mirror, though. His face. Running. Frantic. Screaming at me. All his pretending had fallen away like a thin skin. He was worse than pathetic.'

I drove back to the El Sueño with a monologue running wild in my head. I pictured myself busting in on J.D., ripping him from his bed, and throwing him off the balcony for what he'd done to Lola and the unsuspecting wife. I went into a long tirade on the theme of deception. I rehearsed it out loud and tried desperately to find the right voice. The one I wished for was Richard Burton's. His was the ultimate voice of bitter, self-righteous indignation. Somehow it didn't work without that Welsh working-class inflection, and I felt silly even attempting it by myself in the Buick. J.D. would never buy it anyway. I could use the facial gestures, though. The flaring nostrils. The curling lip. I practiced in the rearview mirror. I pounded on the dashboard and ranted out the open window, into the wind.

When I knocked on J.D.'s motel door, a grayish woman answered. She had the chain lock on and peeked out at me, squeezing a Boston terrier. The dog kept yapping at me so I could barely make out her words. She had a heavy German accent and told me she'd just checked in and wanted some

75

peace and quiet or she'd call the police. I went down to the office and inquired about J.D. The manager handed me my note that I'd buttoned to J.D.'s shirt. I turned it over and read the message he'd left me on the back: ABANDON- MENT IS NO PICNIC, PAL! I'M HEADING FOR VANCOUVER. J.D.

4/10/89 (LOS ANGELES)

Once

She was a tall Scandinavian type from the Iron Range country of Minnesota, who used to sit hunched over at the bar to make her frame look smaller. She was always surrounded with short, dark-haired women wearing nose rings and capes and calling themselves poets. Women who were so opposite to her in every respect that they appeared to be like a pack of dogs surrounding a young deer. They'd plunk dollars' worths of quarters in the Wurlitzer and play only old Hank Williams tunes, then seek out the farthest red booth in the corner, where they'd haul this tall northern girl and then plague her with their latest 'odes' to street madness. Angry Women for Peace, we always called them. I used to watch the tall girl as she moved across the green linoleum floor, balancing an Irish coffee in the palm of her hand and smiling directly at me with an openness that had the slightest edge of melancholy to it. It was this melancholy and the absolute directness of her gaze that first attracted me. Plus her long, athletic legs. She told me she was a dancer, but the way it came across, she'd told the same thing to other men and was waiting for some kind of reaction from me, so I never gave her one. I'd delay her at the bar, while, through her yellow hair, I could see the group of grim-faced bitches champing at the bit, smoking ferociously and giving me the evil eye. They wanted her like a dog wants a bone.

This tall one would sit there coaxing the whipped cream with her tongue and dabbing her index finger into the green stripe of crème de menthe on her drink, as she told me softly about her kind parents and life in the frozen North: skating, falling through ice, moose, fishing on the Great Lakes. She hadn't been in San Francisco long, she said, but she'd been there long enough to know she didn't fit. Her aloneness drew me closer, and I knew this had to be why the poet girls kept circling her. She belonged to herself, something they would never experience. She turned to me and looked right in my face. She said she had a place at the top of Mason, on the ground floor. A basement place, actually, with a window right on the sidewalk. She told me to meet her there if I wanted to and to knock on the window. Don't go to the door, because there was no buzzer and she'd never hear me knocking.

When I got there the window was wide open and the bay breeze was blowing the pages of the *Chronicle* at the foot of her bed. I couldn't see her in there, but I could hear her flat voice inviting me to climb on through. It was her plain, straightforward voice, with no hint of false seduction or double-dealing. Midwestern. I'd never climbed through a sidewalk window before. It felt slightly illegal.

Just before we made love, she told me it was her time of the month and she was very likely to get pregnant since she wasn't using any protection. Neither was I. She said she didn't care. She wanted a baby. She wouldn't bother me about it. She wouldn't hold me responsible or anything. She just wanted to make love and get pregnant. That was all. Her voice never changed.

When I held her I knew she was telling the truth about being a dancer. She was solid muscle right down through her thighs. Muscle like a racehorse has, with nothing extra. She was even longer than I imagined. Every bit as long as me. Our cold feet met evenly at the bottom as we locked up solid and the wind kept clipping the pages of the newspaper at the foot of her bed. This was the one and only time for us, although neither one of us could have known that then.

More than two years passed before I saw her again. I'd think about her now and then and wander back into that bar on the slim chance she might be sitting there, hunched over her Irish coffee, but she never was. Her poet friends would glare at me from their habitual red corner, and one of them even spit in my direction once, but she was too far away to do any damage.

One morning I went into a bookstore on Stockton Street, looking for a copy of *Hunger*, and there was this little blond kid running down the aisle, with a dark-haired woman chasing him, calling him something like 'Nate.' She reached the kid and swooped him up to her chest, laughing wildly. Then she turned and saw me standing there. Her face turned black with rage. 'So this is where you hide!' she said to me in a low growl, then rushed outside, with the little boy squashed in her grip.

I stepped out into the drizzling street and saw the woman running with the boy in her arms. At the corner she handed him over to another woman: a tall blonde who kept looking back over her shoulder at me as the first woman hustled her away. I followed them for a while, but they broke into a trot and dodged cars, crossing the street in a frantic zig-zag. I stopped and watched them go. The tall one never looked back at me after that, but even over the distance, I could see the dark one's eyes trying hard to stab me through the chest.

5/3/95 (SCOTTSVILLE, VIRGINIA)

The
Devouring
Lion

I seem to be fitting in quite well, so they tell me, after my big earthquake of a month ago. They've allowed me back on the farm, and Percer even entrusted me with the big John Deere yesterday. It was a real thrill operating the backhoe again, even with the added burden of trying to keep track of my rampaging thoughts. Following Saint Peter of Damask's precepts of watchfulness and attempting to guard the intellect from the 'Devouring Lion,' I found myself lost in the past more often than not. By systematically punching my thigh now and then, I found I could bring myself back to the task at hand. I'd return to the great teeth of the mechanical bucket, realizing how much my physical technique in controlling the hydraulic levers had atrophied. I could remember a time when they'd felt like an absolute extension of my arms and fingers, and of course, these memories would send me off into the past again. A past full of muscle and youth. I saw with a certainty that it was my own violence that had cut me off from all my old skills. The bucket would scoop too deep, causing the ditch to backfill and run upstream against the creek. I'd try to correct for this by pushing mud back into the cut, but the mistake had already been made. One little slip like this compounds into total disaster, having the exact opposite effect of the original intention. The whole bottom field began to flood, and the panic it inspired in me only caused my efforts to worsen. Slowly the water rose to the driving platform and soon engulfed my boots above the ankle. The crankcase seized up, making it impossible to drop down into the low gear ratio, so there I was, spitting black mud all over the fenceline and sinking deeper with each revolution of the giant wheel. Finally, I cut the engine and sat there staring down as the silty creek water swirled over the top of my boots and inched its way up to my knees. I was not afraid at that point, I must tell you. I knew the level of the water would never reach my neck, so there was no danger of drowning. Someone would find me there eventually. Probably Percer. Of course, this would mean he would never let me get near the tractor again, but at least I would be saved. They'd bring one of the canoes out or something and get me out of there.

Night was falling and the water level had settled just below my waist, so I climbed up on top of the roll bar and took a perch there. I couldn't see anyone up near the barns, and nobody'd rung the dinner bell yet, but I could hear children somewhere, yelling wildly in the distance like they were chasing each other. I don't know why, but I couldn't find the voice to yell back at them. I couldn't find any voice at all.

It was the idea of snakes that prevented me from testing the water for the longest time. I'd seen them lurking under the bridge many afternoons when me and Tyner used to fish there for brim. Big, leather-colored snakes the size of bullwhips. I don't know what kind they were, but I knew they'd chase anything that hit the water. I'd seen them go after dogs before, and the dogs always swam frantically for shore. They never turned to challenge them.

By now my whole body was shaking uncontrollably from the cold setting in. It reminded me of the convulsions I used to go through that first time we were separated, back there in Seguin. Do you remember that time? I was convinced I'd never see you again, and the pain was worse than grieving the death of a parent. I'd rather face snakes than repeat that kind of torture, so I braved the dark water. As I half swam and tripped my way through the debris, I was thinking of you; nothing but you.

I don't suppose you stayed in that place long, though, after what happened. How could you? It would be like inhabiting the rooms of the dead. I don't suppose you even went back to pick up your things. I only hope the animals got taken care of by someone who might have noticed we'd abandoned ship. Actually, I miss nothing from there, if missing means a sense of not being able to live without it. I've learned the dangers of that. After all, it was the missing of you that caused this whole flood to begin with.

11/6/92 (SCOTTSVILLE, VIRGINIA)

Faraway
Lillie

In 1890, on the very skirt of frontier Texas, Judge Roy Bean
fell madly in love with a photograph of the English actress
Lillie Langtry, known worldwide as 'The Jersey Lily.' There
were few women to speak of in that unforgiving country
except for the painted ladies who preyed on the tent camps
of construction workers for the Southern Pacific railroad.
Lawlessness of every stripe was rampant along the Pecos and
Rio Grande border, and the closest legal authority was one
hundred miles away in Fort Stockton. The railroad and the
rangers were desperate for an arbiter, so they appointed a
store proprietor in the tent town of Vinegaroon as their
justice of the peace. Roy Bean was a stocky, dour little man
with slightly wistful eyes and a full white beard. His
autocratic nature made him perfect for the job, and soon his
word became the undisputed law west of the Pecos. To
enforce it he devised the harshest of penalties – not hanging,

but expulsion into that vast wasteland with no gun, no money, no boots, and, worst of all, no horse.

Roy Bean had a pet black bear named Bruno, chained to the steps in front of his makeshift courthouse, which also served as a billiard hall, saloon, and general store. Judge Bean would sometimes confide in his bear after a quick session in 'court' and then ask the bear if he felt justice had been served. Bruno would paw at the dusty steps and snort, then the judge would turn away satisfied, climb into his one-horse gig, and drive off to a quiet place on the river. Here, in the shade of an ancient mesquite, he would compose his letters to the faraway Lillie. He would send her news from the wild frontier. Daily tidbits on men he'd sentenced, for minor offenses like dropping scorpions down a prostitute's blouse to major ones like horse thieving. He bragged to her how he was planning to stage a world-championship prizefight on Rio Grande Sand Flat in defiance of U.S., Mexican, and ranger authority. How he, Roy Bean, had become God in his own little country and how he worshiped her image and longed to meet her some fine spring day. He would pause now and then in his writing to pull out the well-worn photo from his vest pocket and savor her profile. The downcast eyes; the powerful aquiline nose, not unlike his own; the slightly parted lips, as though she were about to whisper his name. Once, he thought he actually heard her voice. Heard her speak to him directly. His whole body jumped, causing his carriage horse to spook, and he very nearly lost the precious photo in the Texas wind. Countless letters he wrote to her in this way, as though he were in dialogue with her, as though she were sitting right there next to him on the buggy seat. He never got an answer. He wrote her that he had named his courthouse and saloon The Jersey Lily in her honor, but he never got an answer. He wrote her that he had hung a reproduction of her portrait by

John Millais over the bar and decorated the corners of the frame with cactus flowers. He'd done the decorating himself. He wrote her that no man was allowed to sit at the bar beneath her portrait wearing a hat or a gun. He received no answer. Finally, after fourteen years of unfulfilled obsession, he wrote her that he had renamed the entire town and that it was now known as Langtry, Texas. *This* got her attention. Lillie Langtry paused momentarily on a transcontinental rail tour in her private 'palace car,' complete with chandeliers, Persian carpets, and lacquered paneling depicting scenes of the Wild West. The 'Sunset Route' of the Southern Pacific was now complete, and the tracks stretched from New Orleans clear to the golden shores of San Francisco. Lillie descended from her car, and as her satin heels pierced the dusty streets of Langtry, she was informed that the good judge had died a month earlier. His successor, however, wanted to present her with Roy Bean's gavel and rifle as gifts in his fond memory. She accepted them both and continued on her way.

7/4/94 (LANGTRY, TEXAS)

Quick
Stop

Do you want to turn back and head home? We could do that if you want.

Why would I want to go home?

I don't know.

We've come this far. How many miles have we come anyway?

Not too many. Three hundred, maybe. That's all.

Three hundred? We've done more than that.

Well, maybe four.

That's a lot. That's a lot to turn around and go back.

I know, but if you're not having a good time there's no point in going on.

I'm fine.

You hungry?

There's not going to be anything open now.

That Exxon had a little Quick Stop connected to it, I think.

What Exxon?

That one just off the interstate. Right there at the exit, where we got off.

You're not going all the way back to the highway, are you?

If you're hungry I will.

What do you mean, if *I'm* hungry? You're the one that's hungry.

Yes, I am. I'm starving, as a matter of fact.

What're they gonna have at the Exxon?

I don't know. Tortilla chips. Chili dogs. Whatever.

No, thanks.

Well, I think I'll head back there and pick up something.

You're going to eat just to eat?

Well – just some potato chips, maybe.

Great. You're going to just leave me here.

Just for a second. I'll be right back.

Are you *that* hungry?

I'm pretty darn hungry.

We just ate about an hour ago.

We did?

Can't you remember? We stopped at the Dairy Queen. Another one of your favorites.

That was just for a malt, though.

How much do you need? All I've had is some carrot juice since we left home. That's all I've had.

Your system is purer than mine.

It's not a question of pure.

I've become dependent on protein. I've been driving all day.

You don't need protein to drive.

It won't take me two seconds to run down there and run back.

You're going to stop and have a drink, I bet. That's it, isn't it? It's got nothing to do with hunger.

All right, look. I'm going to run down to the Exxon, pick up a roast beef sandwich or something – something good and healthy – and then I'm going to turn around and head right straight back here. Now, do you want something to eat or not?

I'm fine.

It was dark now on the frontage road as he passed an Indian family in an old Ford pickup with about seven kids piled in the back. Two older boys were standing with their hands braced on the roof of the cab and their long black hair blowing straight out behind them like crows' wings. The driver looked like he might be their grandfather. That was the only vehicle he passed. Sheet lightning revealed neat rows of round bales and a herd of white-and-tan longhorns, as though they were suddenly standing in bright daylight, then vanishing back into the blackness. The whole flat horizon lit up and blinked silver and gold, but there was no sound of thunder. No rain. He peeked in his rearview mirror to see if the two Indian boys might have turned around to watch his car go by, but the truck had gone. When his eyes shifted back to the road, the center stripe had disappeared. He felt like he was falling. Just for a second.

7/2/91 (KADOKA, SOUTH DAKOTA)

Hail from
Nowhere

When he returned to room number 33, the screen door was propped open by the maid's laundry cart. He could hear a vacuum cleaner going inside, and the maid didn't bother to turn it off when he walked in on her. 'Did you see my wife?' he asked her.

'What's that?'

'My wife! Did you see her when you came in to do the room? Blond hair.'

'Nope, sure didn't. Room was empty. That's why I'm in here. I don't walk into occupied rooms.'

'Well, did you happen to see her leave?'

'Didn't see a soul. Say, who broke this mirror anyhow?'

'I have no idea,' he said as he passed her and took a sideways glance at the long jagged crack in the full-length mirror.

'Somebody's gonna have to pay for the damages, ya know. Wasn't like that yesterday. I'm in here every day like clockwork, and it sure as shootin' wasn't like that yesterday. We take inventory, ya know. Most people don't know that.' He went into the bathroom and pulled the shower curtain back. He checked the sink counter. Her toothbrush, comb, and nail file were right where she'd left them. He brushed past the maid and went back outside to check in the Buick. Maybe she was sitting out there, waiting for him. 'Room was empty when I came in,' the maid babbled on. 'I don't go into rooms unless they're empty.' His heart was going now. There was no sign of her. He turned in a small circle beside his car, tapping his forehead as though trying to prime it for clear thinking. Maybe she just took a walk or something. Went out for some fresh air. This wasn't necessarily a sign of anger. They'd had some kind of a fight, but he couldn't remember the dialogue; couldn't remember the gist of it. He wandered off toward the playground area in a kind of trance, then stopped and stared at the pool for a while. The water confused him. It had a green tinge to it, like it belonged in the wild. His head was throbbing, and he thought he heard a young girl laughing and then the sound of a splash, a body hitting the water, but no one was in the pool. He turned again and wandered back toward the room and stopped by his car. He stared into the dark motel room and watched the maid working systematically, back and forth in front of the tall mirror. A sunbeam was bouncing off the crack, causing a strobe effect each time she passed in front of it. It gave him a sickening sensation, as though daylight was mocking him, indifferent to his crisis. The wind picked up a Styrofoam cup and skipped it across the dirt parking lot. He heard the splash again and turned back toward the pool. A slim, black-haired girl broke the surface and shook the water out of her ears. She had Indian bones but bright green eyes, which smiled directly at him. There was no mistake. She was looking straight at him. She seemed to have no idea he was in a state of emergency. He turned away from her and reentered the room. 'Would you mind leaving now?' he asked the maid, who kept doggedly at her task. 'I need to use the phone.'

'I'll be done in a minute. Still need to change the towels.'

'Just get out,' he said. 'Please.'

'You want dirty towels?'

'I don't care about the towels. My wife is missing, and I need to use the phone.'

'I'll be done in a minute.'

'Just get out! Now!'

'All right. All right. Dirty towels. That's fine by me too.' He picked up the phone as the maid gathered an armload of sheets and stomped out, dragging the Hoover behind her. 'Someone's gonna have to pay for that mirror, ya know. Wasn't like that yesterday.' She snapped the door shut. He rested the phone on his knee and tried to remember the fight. The words to the fight. It had to have been about something. He wondered if he should call the police or the nearest hospital. Maybe it was too soon for that. He'd only left her an hour ago. What was the fight about? Why this mounting panic? It was just another one of their little disagreements. Nothing monumental.

He dropped the phone and went back outside to his Buick. The maid was fiddling with the ice machine and started right in as soon as she spotted him: 'You're not leavin' town by any chance, are you? We've got yer license plate number, ya know. We can always track you down.' As he fired up the engine and backed out of the space marked with a faded white number 33, he caught a glimpse of the black-haired girl in his rearview mirror. She was treading water and smiling straight at him again. This time she waved, her long, thin arm stretched high above her head, as though the distance between them was vast.

He circled the motel slowly and checked inside the laundry/game room. One of the dryers was making a clicking sound and giving off a hot smell of cotton. There were yellow handwritten notes taped to the Kung Fu and Donkey Kong games, which read: *Do not play machines if you are wet! You might become electrocuted!* Some wild part of his imagination had hoped these notes were from his wife.

He checked with the people in the office and took a quick look through the coffee shop. A ranch family were lined up at the cash register, waiting to pay for their breakfast. The men were passing the bill around, questioning each other about who had extra bacon and who had biscuits, as they sucked on toothpicks and dug in their pockets for change.

He drove out Highway 23, past the Bar Dee Bar, and started cutting back up all the little side streets, past dusty front yards where boys practiced their roping on dummy steers. Yapping blue-heelers attacked the Buick as he crept by, craning his neck for any sight of her. She'd pulled this stunt on him before, taking off without notice. Once he'd found her sitting on a curb in front of a doughnut shop, staring at the asphalt. She'd told him she was hunting for agates. They hadn't fought back then. At least he couldn't remember them not getting along. She just took it into her head to wander off.

He crossed the railroad tracks and circled the grain elevators, where all the wheat trucks were lined up to deliver their loads. Some of the drivers waved at him, but he didn't respond. He couldn't figure out why everyone in this town kept waving at him. He didn't know a soul.

He searched down the long gravel roads that snaked out into the wheat and barley fields, hoping to see her. He kept imagining her walking away from him like a Wyeth farm girl, dressed in pink. All he saw were green and yellow combines crawling along the horizon line against an ominous bank of black clouds; so black, in fact, that he thought it might be smoke rolling toward him. He stopped the car and stared as the cloud bank began to rise and separate into long ropy columns swirling out toward the north. In the very center of the darkest column was a whirling gray ball with long strings trailing from it. It seemed to grow in size and kept tumbling down out of the black background, gaining speed while the strings of white stretched out longer and longer, until the whole thing took on the shape of a gigantic octopus dancing across the prairie. The wind suddenly kicked up out of nowhere and rocked the Buick in violent bursts. Broken fence posts tangled in barbed wire cartwheeled across the road in front of him. The temperature dropped so fast he thought something had gone haywire with his air conditioning. Then came the hail. First it came in little clacking flurries that attacked the car from the left, strafing across the hood and peppering the windshield. He didn't recognize the sound at first. It reminded him of showers of Dove Shot falling through pine trees. Then everything accumulated and descended with a vengeance. From out of nowhere, huge baseball-size frozen rocks came slamming into him from all sides. He cut the engine off and gripped down on the wheel. He couldn't see the road anymore. He could barely make out the hood ornament. It kept right on coming at him as he frantically rolled the windows up and hung on dumbly to the wheel as though that were somehow going to save him. The Buick rolled from side to side like a tiny helpless ship caught on the edge of a hurricane. He could make out the faint headlights of the grain trucks as they blinked warnings to each other of their whereabouts. He switched on his hazard lights, but all they produced was a fuzzy glowing pulse in the darkening swirl. The whole back window suddenly exploded into a spiderweb, and he ducked down, seeking protection under the dashboard. The deep, howling whine of the wind came up at him through the floorboards, and he felt a sickening anxiety that this was it. This was how it was going to end for him and her. Not in the sunlight, facing the granite faces of Mount Rushmore, buying postcards and sipping iced tea. Not reconciled and reunited, but totally lost and apart and dead somewhere, by an act of God.

As suddenly as it had started up, the hailstorm broke and disappeared. The sun came out hot and wide open. There wasn't a trace in the sky of what had just taken place. The grain trucks had vanished, leaving a wake of crushed white sludge in their tire tracks. A meadowlark called from a distance as though asking permission to continue its life. Pyramids of frozen hailstones lay stacked against every tree and fence post. What could their fight have possibly been about?

He returned to room 33 with the certainty that she wouldn't be there. She wouldn't be sitting on the edge of the bed, purse in lap, biting her lip. She wouldn't leap up and throw herself into his arms when he entered the door. He was right. He went straight to the phone and called the nearest hospital. They had no record of her. All their newest corpses were Indian. He called the local police department, and they told him the sheriff wasn't in but to come by and fill out a missing persons form. He felt it was still too soon for that. He couldn't quite bring himself to regard her as 'missing' in the broadest sense. 'Missing' like she'd never be found. He gave them a description of her, and as he was listing the color of her eyes and hair, her weight and height, her age – all these ordinary details seemed to pull him further away from her, until he had a hard time even picturing her face. 'Well, we'll send an APB out on her, sir, but you really need to come down and fill out the forms.'

He called her mother in Wisconsin, and her voice

sounded so frail and distant that he felt compelled to make up a story about her daughter's sudden absence, telling her they must have misunderstood each other about a meeting place.

'I just wondered if she might have called you or something.'

'No, I haven't heard a thing,' she said.

'Well, she's bound to show up sooner or later. How's the weather up there?'

'We're having a cold snap.'

'It's the middle of summer.'

'Not here it isn't.' She laughed with a kind of sweet resignation that caused his whole heart to sink.

'Just went through a hailstorm here. Very freakish.'

'Hail?'

'Yeah. Just came up out of the blue. Never seen anything like it.'

'We rarely have that here. Hail.'

'Well, I'll be sure to call you as soon as she shows up.'

'I can't understand that. Unless she's gone off on one of her long walks. You know how she does.'

'I wouldn't worry. She'll turn up.'

He signed off awkwardly, not sure whether her mother had wandered away from the phone or was in the process of hanging up. He sat there on the edge of the bed, staring at the phone. He stood up and moved toward the bathroom but stopped in front of the long mirror and stared at the split image of himself caused by the crack. She had to have made that crack in some sudden rage. An ashtray, maybe? Her little fist?

He moved into the bathroom and took off his shoes and socks, rolled up his pant legs, then turned on the cold water and stepped into the tub. He let the water run over his toes and stared down at his feet. His neck and shoulders began to take on an attitude that reminded him of his wife. The same posture of melancholy; slumped slightly, with the arms hanging limply at his sides. This was her body; her expression of despair. About what? What was at the heart of it? He felt the pull downward, his eyes sinking deeper into the veins of his feet. The weight of fatigue caused by years of mourning. For what? He was slipping now; drawn deeper inside her until he actually felt he was becoming her. He was closer to her now in her absence, than he'd ever been when he was with her. He knew something about her for the first time. His breath even took on the same rhythm as hers. He felt his vision close down, until he was no longer seeing his feet on the porcelain. The sound of the tap water became dull and distant, and the weight of his head slowly drew his chin down into his chest. He felt buried inside this form, smothered by it. He gasped like a child thrown into icy water and grabbed hold of the plastic shower curtain, tearing it down as he fled the bathroom toward the queen-size bed. He threw himself facedown on the bedspread, with its faded pattern of prairie schooners surrounded by Indians, and the sound of the weeping that came out of him scared some part of himself, but he couldn't stop. He lost any semblance of controlling it. His whole body was involved.

It was some time before he began to regain himself. He just lay there with his face cocked toward the window. He could hear the bathtub still running and, outside, the sound of sprinklers. He managed to swing his cold feet toward the door. He stood and didn't bother to unroll his pant legs. He moved toward the door and felt crusty patches on the red carpet where somebody must have puked in the past. He stepped outside into the scorching sun.

He crossed the parking lot, barefooted, toward a sprinkler that was throwing pathetic half-circles of water on a little swatch of grass by the pool. The spray was causing a short blue rainbow to appear and disappear against the sun. He walked straight into the arc of water and let it slap across his neck. He stood there, waiting for the next pass, knowing his body would jump when it came. There was nothing he could do about it. A voice spoke directly behind him, and at first he thought it might be coming from inside his head. 'I used to do that when I was a little kid.' He turned and looked into the green eyes peering at him out of her powerful face.

'I don't know you, do I?' His voice came out like a little boy's.

'I don't know.' She giggled. '*Do* you?'

'But how come you were waving at me before?'

'I just saw you and waved. That's all. A person can wave, can't they?' The sprinkler was slapping them both now, and she laughed when he ducked from it. 'What're you doing out here?' she said.

'Vacation. Just a little vacation.'

'No, I mean why are you standing out here in the sprinkler all by yourself, with your pants rolled up?'

'Oh. I've just lost my wife,' he said, and shook water out of his hair with a quick jerk. She started laughing so hard she doubled over and slapped her knees, then she spun around and faced him. When she saw his expression, she stopped and wiped the smile off her face with the back of her hand.

'Sorry,' she said.

'About what?'

'For laughing. It just seemed funny when you said that about your wife and then you did that thing with your head.'

'What thing?'

'That flip thing. You know.' Then she demonstrated the gesture for him, whipping her head to one side.

'Oh,' he said.

'It just made it seem like – I don't know. Anyway, I'm sorry.'

'Like what?'

'I don't know. Like she was dispensable or something.'

'Oh.'

'Is she?'

'What?'

'Dispensable?'

'She's gone.'

'Did she die or something?'

'No. She disappeared.'

'Nobody disappears.'

'She did.'

'How'd she manage that?'

'She's just gone.'

'Maybe she went shopping.'

'She never shops.'

'Well, maybe she went up to visit the Petrified Gardens.'

'What's that?'

'You know, the Petrified Gardens. That's the only reason anyone stops here.'

'Oh.'

'Why'd you stop here?'

'I don't know. Vacation. Actually, we were having a little disagreement in the car.'

'Oh. A fight?'

'No, just a little misunderstanding.'

'What was that about?'

'I can't remember.' He stared down at his bare feet, which now had a pattern of mud up to his ankles.

'Well, have you looked for her?'

'Yeah. Of course I looked for her. I've searched all over town. Got caught in that hailstorm looking for her.'

'That was a doozy, wasn't it. Happens all the time, this time of year. They just come out of nowhere.'

'I've never seen anything like it.'

'Do you want me to help you look for her? I was born and raised here. I know every inch of it.'

'No, that's all right.'

'Why not?'

'Because – I mean, I don't even know you. I don't know who you are. You just walk up to me and – You waved at me like you knew me or I knew you or something, but I *don't* know you. I don't have the slightest idea who you are. I don't understand how you can just – I don't know. It doesn't make any sense. I mean, losing something – losing someone – and then, here you are. I don't – I have no idea –'

'About what?'

'About where to begin.'

7/2/91 (KADOKA, SOUTH DAKOTA)

Just
Space

No, Mama, I'm still in South Dakota.

Oh, that's right. Your beau called me from out there.

He did? What did he want?

He said he'd lost you temporarily.

He's not my 'beau,' Mama; he's my husband.

Oh, that's right.

And it's not temporary either. It's forever.

What is?

The loss.

Oh. Well, when are you coming back home, then?

I've got a job out here now. I'm working again.

Why are you doing that?

We've separated. I need to make some money.

You and your beau?

My husband, Ma!

You're not together?

That's right. We've separated. Forever. I just told you.

When did all this happen?

Few days ago. Actually, it's been going on for quite a while.

What has?

The split.

Oh, I didn't know that. I didn't realize.

Yeah. Anyhow, I'm working again.

Well, what line of work are you following now?

I'm working at the Happy Chef.

What's that?

Restaurant, Mama. I'm a waitress again.

Happy Chef. Never heard of that one.

They have them out here. Not out there.

Never heard of it. What's it like – a Dairy Queen or something?

Something like that. Yeah.

You were never that before, were you? A waitress?

Yeah. Don't you remember, up by the lakes that one summer?

Oh. That was a long time ago, wasn't it.

I guess so.

I don't remember you being a waitress up there, though.

Yeah. I had a blue uniform, remember? This one's brown.

Which one?

This one I've got on right now. I wear it all the time. I really like it a lot. I've got a brand-new nameplate too, with a brand-new name.

What do you mean, a new name?

Rita. I've changed my name to Rita Olsen.

What kind of a name is that?

Half Spanish, half Swedish. I just came up with it.

You're not Spanish *or* Swedish.

I know. I just invented it.

Well, you can't change your name like that, can you? Just out of the blue.

Why not?

Why would you want to change your name at this late date?

It's just a disguise.

Disguise?

So he can't find me.

He's been looking for you?

He tried to shoot me.

No! Good Lord!

He did. He shot a hole right through my windshield.

Are you all right?

Yeah, sure. He missed me by a mile. You know, all those guns he always drags around with him, and he can't even shoot straight.

Well, did you report him to the police?

No. He won't try it again.

How can you be sure about that?

I've just got a feeling.

Well, I think you ought to have him arrested. He can't just go around shooting at people. That's not right.

Things are different out here.

When are you coming back home?

I don't know, Mama.

Why are you dating a man who carries guns anyway? I thought you were smarter than that.

I'm not dating him! I'm married to him! Don't you remember?

No.

We got married a long time ago. We got married out here, as a matter of fact. It was in the spring.

I remember you going out there on a train, but I don't remember any man.

We came back and lived with you for three months. Me and him.

Oh, that's right. But he was very sweet. That one. That's not the same man who carries guns, is it?

Yeah. It's the same one.

Why would he want to carry guns? He seemed so sweet.

He's crazy.

No. It's not the same man, then, because the man I remember you bringing home used to help with the dishes and the fire-wood. He was always bringing me things from the store. He shoveled snow off the driveway that one winter when we had that bad blizzard. You remember?

No.

That couldn't be the same man, because I remember telling you that was the man you ought to marry. But you wouldn't listen to me.

That's the man I *did* marry!

I remember saying you'll never find another one like that one in a million years. Someone who takes care of you and watches out for the house.

I've gotta go, Mama.

Where are you going now?

I've got to get ready for work.

What time is it there?

We're an hour ahead of you.

You work at night?

Yeah. I'm a waitress. I like it. I get to sleep all day.

You should come home.

I might.

You don't belong out there. What's out there anyway?

Just – space. I guess.

We've got that here. There's space here.

It's not the same.

Don't change your name, whatever you do. It's a sin to do that.

I've got to go, Mama.

Please don't change your name.

It's just temporary, Mama.

7/91 (KADOKA, SOUTH DAKOTA)

Pure Accident

He lay flat on his back on the red rug, staring up at the lumpy ceiling. He figured it must have been some kind of fire retardant they'd sprayed up there; like moldy cottage cheese, ready to fall on his head any second. He was getting lost in details. Details of his immediate environment. It seemed a safe bet to him. Enclosed; where hail couldn't hit him. He might never leave this room again. He studied patterns of shadows on the wall created by the sun throwing light through the folds of the plastic curtains. He watched them move and shift and thought about how difficult it would be to draw them accurately. Even in black and white. He listened to voices in other rooms; just the sounds of voices, without being able to make out the words. Two men laughing, with the TV going full blast. TV in daytime. Baseball. Two men laughing; wishing they were with women instead. Any women. A distant lawn mower – somebody working to improve his tiny patch of real estate.

The ice machine. The distant road. Then the sun suddenly shifted and washed all the shadows away in a cool, gray light. His back was aching, and he thought it must be from all the driving he'd done. All the driving he'd ever done. Miles he could never begin to account for; crisscrossing the country for reasons he'd long lost track of. Driving just to be driving. He pictured a map of the country on the lumpy ceiling, with Canada and Mexico amputated into black space; an island continent. Then, threading from coast to coast and north to south, were clusters of long, spiraling yellow lines, representing all his past trips. Trips without consequence, as far as he could remember. Except the one where he'd first met her. That line was red and began in Salt Lake at the state fair. They were standing right next to each other, watching a mule show. Total strangers. It was pure accident. They were both so hypnotized by the vision of flying mules diving off a hundred-foot platform that they never even noticed each other. The mules would land in a tank of water with a tremendous belly flop: all four legs stiffened out, eyes terrified, and emitting a god-awful scream as they fell. Finally, one of them missed the tank, and she had thrown herself into his chest, covering her mouth and moaning as though she'd received the impact herself. He held her and patted her back softly. She allowed him to encircle her with his arms. He held her the way he would a frightened child. The crowd was breaking up all around them. The guts of the mule had rolled out into the parking lot, steaming and blue. Attendants were running around with buckets and ropes, screaming orders at one another. He moved her away from the scene, toward a yellow tent in the distance that served hot dogs and beer. She went along with him, as though they belonged together. She crossed her wrists on her chest and kept her chin tucked tightly down on her clenched fists. People were running past them, back toward the accident. High-pitched, excited voices. One of them yelled out that there'd been a murder, and then all the voices rose a notch and more people came running. She stopped suddenly and looked up into his face. 'Oh, I'm sorry,' she said, and went running off. It took him all day to find her again. Then they lived together for five years straight.

7/91 (KADOKA, SOUTH DAKOTA)

Repeat

Now, repeat. Let's get it in our head: 'I am a man, not to be trusted.' Let's repeat.

I am a man, not to be trusted.

Good. 'I am a man to which the truth is an ever-shifting phenomenon.'

I am a man to which – 'To which'?

'To which.' Yes. That's right. 'To which.'

That seems like an odd way to put it.

Just repeat.

'To which'?

'I am a man *to which* the truth is –'

All right. I am a man to which the truth is an ever-changing –

'Ever-shifting.'

Ever-shifting phenomenon.

Very good. 'I am a man bewildered and incapable of remembering –'

I am a man bewildered and incapable –

'Of remembering my many personal disasters.'

I'm an incapable man –

No, no, no! 'I am a man *incapable* –'

I am a man incapable –

'Bewildered and incapable.' Right.

Bewildered and incapable.

'Of remembering –'

Of remembering –

'My many personal –'

My many personal disgraces.

NO! '*Disasters!*' 'My many personal disasters!' Why can't you get this?

What's the matter with 'disgraces'?

'Disgrace' is too light. It carries no weight. If it were simply 'disgrace,' we wouldn't be going through this, would we?

All right. My many personal disasters. Jesus.

That's right. 'I am a man bewildered and incapable of remembering my many personal disasters.'

That's what I said.

Good. 'And therefore I am doomed to repeat them forever and ever into eternity.'

And therefore I am doomed –

'To repeat them forever and ever –'

To repeat them forever and ever –

'Into eternity.'

Repeat what?

My *disasters!* What in the world is wrong with you? Why can't you get this?

Can we take a break now?

No. Absolutely not.

Just a short one.

No!

I need to take a leak.

Not yet. Now repeat: 'I am a man –'

I am a man –

'I am a man who has lost all control of his senses.'

I am a man who has lost all control of his senses.

'All control of his mind.'

All control of his mind.

'All control of his heart.'

All control of his heart.

'All control of his soul.'

All control of his soul.

'And therefore I willingly and earnestly –'

And therefore I willingly and earnestly –

'Turn myself over completely –'

Turn myself over completely –

'To the care and trusted instruction –'

To the care and trusted instruction –

'Of my longtime mentor and personal bodyguard –'

Of my longtime mentor and personal bodyguard – That's you, right?

That's me.

That's what I thought. Can I take a leak now?

Yes, you may.

9/15/94 (LEXINGTON, KENTUCKY)

Dust

Price crept slowly into town, passing a little landmark sign that read: *Belvidere – The Town Too Tough To Die.* He didn't see any town to speak of. An abandoned tire repair shop. An abandoned barbecue joint called Tibbs' Ribs. The only thing not abandoned was a Conoco station with a little café and food shop behind it. He pulled in there and parked. It was still too early for Lowell and his fabulous daughter to show up. The only thing he could remember him saying about the meeting place was the Belvidere turnoff. So this was good enough. He could see the highway exit from where he sat. He watched some aging bikers roll into the parking lot, riding double on giant Jap bikes with little microphones implanted in their helmets, like fat Martians. Their lips were moving, but he couldn't hear any voices. Whatever happened to *The Fugitive Kind?* he wondered. At least they *belong* to something; some Japanese-biker world for fatties. He pulled himself up on the seat and started having second thoughts about this meeting. After all, the only real reason he'd come was just to catch another glimpse of Lowell's daughter. He felt a little guilty about it. As he stuck the key in the ignition, he saw Lowell Hewitt's outfit crest a hill and cross the railroad tracks, heading for the Conoco station. Although Price had never seen Lowell's truck and trailer before, he knew it had to be him. The pickup was an extension of Lowell himself, an old green Ford Ranger so layered in prairie dust and gumbo mud that it had become part of the paint job itself. There weren't two matching tires on the entire rig, including the stock trailer, which was a battered flesh color scarred with huge liver-shaped rust spots dotting the nose and fenders. Three saddled ranch horses were frantically clawing to catch their balance as Lowell fishtailed the trailer into the gas station and slammed on brakes, sending the horses crashing forward, almost to their knees. 'Had yer breakfast yet!' Lowell yelled out the window at him, through the settling dust.

'Yessir!' Price called back, pulling the keys out of the ignition. Madilia's raw face was hidden behind her father's hat brim, but Price caught a glimpse of her, slamming her shoulder into the jammed door on her side, trying to bail out. His heart clicked in his throat.

'That's good, 'cause we won't eat again till sundown! Some fancy outfits hire a Piper Cub to drop lunch, but we're not one of those! Never have been.' Lowell laughed and hawked a rolling gob of tobacco juice in Price's direction as he headed across the gravel toward them. Madilia finally got her door punched open and went around the tailgate of the pickup and hopped the hitch. He was hoping she'd at least take a look at him, but she just strode straight off toward the café, with her hands stuffed in her back pockets. He felt like a teenager, the way his head was heating up. 'Why don't you pile on in with us, Price? No point takin' two vehicles back in there.'

'No, that's all right. I'll just follow.'

'Suit yerself. Yer gonna eat a lotta dust, though. These old washboard roads can really kick it up.'

'That's okay. Doesn't look like you've got much room in there.'

'How much room do ya need?' Lowell jeered, spewing brown Copenhagen slime again. There was an awkward pause where Price found himself turning back toward the little café in anticipation of Madilia's return. He felt caught now and almost wished he were a member of the fat-biker group, waddling off toward their glitzy machines, sucking on gonzo Pepsis. He turned back to Lowell and made a faint attempt at a smile.

'You brought an extra horse, huh?' he said to Lowell.

'You didn't wanna ride double, did ya? Or maybe you did!' Lowell reached out the window of the truck and punched Price's shoulder, then guffawed and pounded on the steering wheel with his other hand. 'That old high cantle she rides'll knock yer dick in the dirt!' He launched into a hacking and spitting fit, while Price rubbed his shoulder, hoping Lowell wouldn't notice that his punch had actually gotten to him a bit. 'You don't wanna mess around with any half-breed women anyhow, Price. Believe you me. They'll eat yer lunch!'

'Why's that?'

'Just lead to big trouble for ya back there in Ioway. Besides, yer married, ain't ya?'

'I'm not from Iowa,' Price said, and he looked up right into Lowell's wide face. Lowell stopped gnawing on his chew and stared at him blankly.

'Thought you said you was from Iowa, or was I half in the bag?'

'Yeah, that's what I said, but I'm not from there. I don't like Iowa – especially Des Moines. Des Moines reminds me of Russia.'

'Well, where the heck are ya from, then?'

'Kentucky,' Price said off the top of his head.

'I'll be darned. Kentucky. Suppose yer not in the fertilizer business either.'

'That's right. I'm not.'

'I'll be doggoned. How 'bout the married part? Yer not makin' that up, are ya, or am I a complete fool?'

'No. That part's true.'

'Well, least we got half a leg to stand on.' Lowell took a long, hard look at Price, then smiled and spit the whole used-up wad of Copenhagen out the window and watched it land like a steaming turd. 'Yer one mixed-up fella, ain't ya, Price?'

Madilia came out of the café, swinging a six-pack of Budweiser in each hand and walking just like Price imagined she would. She didn't smile at him until she got within a few yards of the truck. 'You comin' with us in our outfit?' she asked him as she kept right on striding around to her door.

'No, I'm going to follow.'

'Yer liable to eat a lotta dust.'

'That's what your dad told me.'

'He was right,' she said, just before she slammed the creaking door.

Price tried to keep up with Lowell's rig the best he could on the gravel ranch roads, but the closer he kept to the stock trailer, the less visibility he had through the swirling dust, until he was afraid he'd rear-end them if Lowell had to slam on brakes for some reason. He backed off a good eight or ten car lengths, but Lowell maintained a steady sixty, with the trailer wagging the dog through every turn and the horses scrambling to catch their feet. Price had known dust in his time, but this was beyond description. It poured through every possible crack, through the closed vent and the floorboards. He could taste it and grind it between his teeth. His nose and ears filled up with it. His eyes were caked with a gray crust. The back of his throat was coated with it. His hands turned pale and chalky. The narrow road snaked on and on, and all he could do was follow Lowell's storm and hope some John Deere hay wagon didn't suddenly poke up over a hill at 5 mph, heading in his direction. He began to feel a slight panic at the thought of losing this father-and-daughter team out here in the badlands. He had no clue where the interstate was now, and they'd already forked off at two or three different junctions. Junctions with no signposts or landmarks of any kind. He tried to remember which fork they'd just taken: the left or the right? Exactly how many? Two, he thought. Maybe three but most likely just two. Both to the left. He was almost sure they'd been both to the left. He started straining his eyes through the glass for some kind of distinguishing features, but the buttes in the distance all looked the same through the haze of dust. As soon as he'd fix on a unique, pyramid-shaped one – slate gray with salmon-colored stripes running horizontally through it – then another one would appear, identical to it. He fixed on one out his right window with a long, slender, wind-eroded neck and a knob on top that looked like a hawk's head. He thought *that* one would have to be singular and tried to memorize it as having been seen on his right, but then a twin to it suddenly appeared on his left. He thought he was in Egypt for a second. He saw buffalo turn into camels; shimmering heat bands on the horizon, with dark date palms suddenly jumping out and dancing in a line. All he could do was try to keep up. He accelerated three or four car lengths and resigned himself to the suffocating dust. The dashboard was so thick with it by now that he couldn't see the numbers on the speedometer. Not that speed mattered much. He began to imagine Lowell and his amazing daughter laughing their heads off at him and popping cans of Budweiser up ahead. He could almost see them elbowing each other in the ribs and punching the headliner. He wondered how it was that he'd suddenly become the object of ridicule in the middle of the open plains. His blood started to rise at the thought of it. It was women again. The stupid lure of women. He slammed the Buick down into second, causing the rear end to bite so violently he almost lost total control, but he pulled it back out and hugged the left shoulder. The dust attack was less on that side of the road, but the risk of a head-on slowly pushed him back over to the right again, directly on Lowell's tail. He stared into the jerry-rigged back gate of the horse trailer, a snarled-up network of old rotten ropes and baling wire lashing a slat-board gate in place. He was now face-to-face with the wild-eyed, spread-eagled horses, who had all turned tail and faced the rear, trying to avoid the relentless dust. A dun gelding, closest to the back gate, stared out at him, eyes terrified, nostrils pulsing for air. It was the stare of a plain victim.

After ten miles of this test by dust and gravel, they pulled off into a cedar brake, sheltering a jumble of ancient bleached-out corrals and loading chutes. Price parked by a stump and waited for them to emerge from the Ford. When he cut off the ignition his body kept pulsing, as though the rutted road had somehow gotten up into his bones and would never leave him. He was chewing dirt and spitting whole gobs of it out the window. His lungs burned with it. He could see Madilia repeating the same madness of slamming her shoulder into the truck door. The violence of it, the way she committed her whole body to it, made him wonder how she could have ever had the power to draw him out this far into completely unknown territory. Her father swung his thick legs out. He was wearing the same indelible broad smile and squeezed a beer in his hand. 'What kinda vehicle you call that, Price? Never seen anything like it!'

'Grand National!' Price yelled back, shoveling dust off his shirt and pants with both hands.

'Grand National. The heck. Never heard a that one. Thought that was a horse race over in England!'

'Buick,' Price spat out.

'Keeps up pretty good for a city car.'

'Yeah. Fastest stock car in America now. Turbo.'

'Fastest stock car in America! How 'bout that!' Lowell chuckled and shuffled around to the back gate of the trailer, beginning to untie the maze of frayed rope and wire. He yanked a knot loose with his teeth and held his Bud to the side so it wouldn't get more dust in it.

'You haul those horses kinda fast, don't you, Lowell?' Price said, trying to push himself into the spirit of things.

'Nothin' better for a bronc than a good slam-bang trailer ride. Bounce 'em off the walls a few times, it takes the snot right out of 'em. Makes 'em think twice about crackin' their back with ya.'

'Bronc?'

'Oh, yers is broke. Don't you worry about that. We wouldn't mount ya on nothin' with a cold back. We might look a little rough around the edges, but we aim to please. Yers is a pussycat. Guaranteed.' Lowell flopped open the rickety gate just as Madilia vaulted out of her stuck door and came around to meet them.

'Told ya about the dust,' she said to Price. 'You didn't believe me.'

'I believe you.'

'It'll take the better part of a week to clean all that shit outa yer lungs.'

'Yeah, I suppose,' he said, raking more dirt out of his hair and trying to get his eyes unglued.

As soon as Lowell pried the gate back, the dun gelding who'd been staring at Price on the road came blasting out backward, then jammed both hocks in the ground and flipped completely over, ramming the saddle horn into his withers. Madilia went right after him like a cattle dog, grabbing the loose reins and jerking his head up. She popped him on the ass with the tip of the rein and the dun leaped to all fours and shook himself, with a dismayed look in his eye. He spun around in a tight circle, farting in short staccato bursts and raising more dust. Madilia kept snapping the rein and spinning around with him in a circle while the oxbow stirrups rattled and caught him behind the cinch. The dun leaped straight up in the air, all four feet off the ground, screaming like he'd been struck by lightning. As soon as he landed, Madilia bent his head back around to his shoulder with the rein, slipped her red boot in the stirrup, and swung a leg up over him. The whole thing happened in a blink, and Price thought he might be falling in love again. 'Hard to believe he's got half a dozen rides in him and he's still goosy about the cinch.' Lowell chortled as they both watched his daughter reach back with her spurs and dig the horse deep in the flank, then turn his head loose. The dun jumped out at a wide-open, hell-bent-for-leather gallop, then jammed to a stop and began to buck for all he was worth. 'See what I mean about these half-breed women, Price? You don't wanna mess with 'em.' Lowell laughed and nudged Price's arm with his elbow, then guzzled on his beer as they watched Madilia lay back on the cantle and rake the bronc savagely across the shoulders with both heels. Price just stood there, stupefied. He hadn't seen anything like it since the days of the great Casey Tibbs. 'She'll ride just about anything with hair on it,' Lowell said, and walked back to the trailer, pulling the two other horses out. He handed one set of reins to Price and nodded toward the blue horizon. 'This one here's a veteran. Jest give him his head and point him. He'll do all the rest. Now we best grab leather. We got miles to put on.'

They took off at a killing jog, with Madilia finally getting the dun lined out to a broken, humpbacked trot. Whenever the gelding tried to crack his back with her, she'd dig into him with the spurs again and pop him with her heeling rope. After about a mile and a half of this routine he began to drop his head and give in to the bridle, sweat leaching off his back cinch in frothy white ribbons. Price tried to keep pace, stealing glimpses at Madilia and finding his seat in the old brokendown stock saddle. Her father got after the Budweiser right away, thrashing around in his saddlebags and letting the reins flop. He offered a can out to Price, who politely refused. 'Suit yerself. I find it helps a man git down on a horse's spine jest a little bit better. Horse seems to sense it when a man's stone sober.'

For more than an hour, the three of them never broke out of this jagged, spine-jamming trot. It didn't matter what kind of terrain they covered – sandy creek bottoms, shale slopes, open plains riddled with prairie dog holes – the jog never altered. Price's gelding had a jackhammer stride that rattled every tooth in his head. They crashed through cactus, straight down sheer twelve-foot embankments into thick brush then came out splashing into murky creeks, with unseen boulders and cedar stumps jutting up at them like rusty bayonets. They scrambled up the opposite banks, the ground giving loose in long slabs of crumbling clay; finally gaining footing on the flat tableland above, then weaving through more cactus and sudden holes where whole villages of prairie dogs chirped at them manically as they trespassed in their domain. They jogged on in silence, and the pace never changed. Price felt himself being towed along, not so much by his horse but by Lowell's intent. Price watched him standing long in the stirrups, leaning slightly forward over the horn, hands absolutely still, as he gazed out over his gelding's ears for the herd. It was a gaze that seemed to go back a good two hundred years.

They moved on into higher country and finally reached the top of a long grassy table that offered a clear view in every possible direction. Up till now they hadn't seen a single cow, calf, or yearling, and they must have covered at least eight miles of country. Nothing was out there but the awesome, farflung prairie, which more and more took on the aspect of some foreign planet. He watched Madilia, sitting calmly now in the saddle, with one leg hooked around the saddle horn. Her eyes were following the same line of vision as her father's, out across the vast, sprawling flatland. Lowell was squinting through a miniature pair of camou-flage-green binoculars, the kind you'd buy in an army-surplus store, slowly scanning the horizon from left to right. Not a word had passed between the three of them since they'd left the truck and trailer. It was as if the land itself had put them in their rightful place and stripped the need for idle talk. Price watched Madilia's eyes. He went inside them and fell into a stupid spell about her heritage. He was connecting her directly now to Crazy Horse and the Oglala warrior nation. He was losing himself in the saddle. He had to hold on to keep from keeling over suddenly. Maybe it was the dust and the road fatigue. A sharp scream came out of him. He was sure it was him, although the pitch of it and its sudden eruption gave him the sense he was maybe temporarily possessed. It reminded him of the way a burro will cut loose, for no apparent reason, in the dead of night. His borrowed horse bolted, then locked up solid and pinned his dark ears back, waiting for something even more weird to follow. Madilia slowly turned to him and smiled softly, but Lowell never took his eyes away from the pair of binoculars. Maybe he was deaf, Price thought. There was no denying a scream had come from his throat. 'I was just trying to see how far my voice would carry out here,' he said by way of apology to Madilia, but she just turned her attention back to her father and waited.

'Don't see cow one,' Lowell said softly, eyes still glued to the lenses.

'I bet they're over on the other side of Pipestone,' his daughter replied.

'I'll bet a man could yell his head off out here and nobody'd ever hear him,' Price continued. 'A man could die out here yelling his fool head off.'

'Some have,' Lowell said, as he kept pivoting slowly in the saddle, with both his big meaty hands cradling the glass to his eyes. His elbows were locked solid against his ribs to steady his gaze. 'My guess is they're over there on Red Table. See all this land here, Price? All this yer eyeballin' right now fell under what they called the Homestead Act. Probably the very last Sioux land that fell into white men's hands. Happened back when Ulysses S. Grant became President. You remember him? Whupped the stew outa the South. He's the one opened all this back up for white settlement. Had no business doin' it either, tell ya the damn truth. Broke every treaty in the book. Every promise we ever made. But here we are now, and that's the way it happened. I'm a half-breed myself, so I got no call to be passin' judgment on either side of the fence.' Lowell's pivoting stopped, and he fixed on a distant spot in the immense landscape. He motioned for Price to pull up next to him while he adjusted the focus on the lenses. 'Price, I want you to see somethin' here. Come on up here alongside me.' Price nudged his horse up next to Lowell's and took the binoculars, as Lowell placed his massive hand on the back of Price's neck to guide his vision. It made Price feel like he was about nine years old. He was afraid he might cry out again, for no reason, or break down in some terribly injured part of himself that was forever missing a father. 'You see that gray knob just below the rim of that table out there? Out past the reef. You know what that is?' Price tried to focus through the tiny eyepieces, but all he saw was a distant wall of rock, fringed with scrub pine. 'I'll bet ya dollars to doughnuts there's a buffalo skull buried in that knob. You can tell by the color. See how it's kinda yellowish around the edges? That's the horn bone stickin' out.' Price wanted desperately to see this apparition but couldn't nail it down. 'We're gonna ride on over there and dig it out. It's on our way anyhow. You can take it back home with ya as a souvenir. Hang it on yer wall and brag on it some, back there in Ioway or wherever it is you come from.'

'Kentucky.'

'Kentucky, then. They got many buffalo in Kentucky?'

'I believe they used to.'

'Then it oughta be a real conversation piece for ya.'

They resumed their jog as Lowell returned the binoculars to his saddlebag and fished for another beer. He offered one out to Price again but got the same refusal.

'Whatsa matter? Budweiser's not yer brand?'

'No; I just bloat up on beer.'

'Kentucky bourbon must be yer game, huh?'

They descended the steep wall of the high table, down into the grassland floor. Lowell turned himself all the way around in the saddle to speak to Price, mashing his big hand down on the horse's rump. 'Me and the daughter have made some strange discoveries out here. Found us an old buffalo robe in a cave once that had three carbines wrapped up in it. All rusted out and the stocks were eaten away by the wind, but they dated back to the 1890s.'

'No kidding.'

'Found a locket too, with an old faded photograph of a young girl. Couldn't hardly make out the face, but there was a shank of yellow hair in there with it. Hair like silk. Musta been an old hideout. Badlands've always been famous for hiding outlaws and such.'

'I suppose so.'

'Yer not hidin' out, are ya, Price?' As Lowell asked him this he turned back toward the head of his horse and kept pointing him straight down the slope, sipping on his beer. Price felt a slight electric sting go through him from the question.

'No; why?'

'Don't make a damn bit a difference to me. A man's a man till he proves himself otherwise.'

'Why would I be hiding out?'

'Beats the hell outa me. None a my business anyhow. Lotta loose ends, though. You gotta admit.'

'How do you mean?'

'Well, like I said, it ain't my business, but you don't seem to know where the hell you come from or where yer goin', do ya, Price?' Lowell spurred his horse into a jump and loped the rest of the way down the sharp incline, beer-laden saddlebags popping up and down with every stride. Price kept picking his way carefully and watched Lowell as he finally hit the basin at a full gallop and kept right on spurring, while balancing his can of beer out to the side.

'Lotta loose ends? What's that supposed to mean?' Price asked himself out loud as he studied the steep footing directly in front of him. Madilia drew up alongside him, laughing and pointing at her father, far below, racing across the yawning basin like something out of a Remington painting.

'He's about one day away from the wild, isn't he! Lookit that! Born a hundred years too late in his problem.'

'Guess so.'

'That horse workin' out all right for ya?'

'Yeah. He's fine. A little choppy, but that's okay.'

'He's not too much for ya, is he?' She laughed.

'No. He's just perfect.'

''Cause we can swap if you want. This one's all trained now.' She grinned at him with all her Lakota teeth flashing

'No, thanks. This one's fine.' They edged their way down, two abreast, for a while, then Madilia turned to him, shifting her weight back in the saddle. 'What was that scream you let out back there? That yowl.'

'What? Oh. That wasn't a scream exactly.'

'What was it, then?'

'I told you – I was just testing my voice a little.'

'Testing your voice? Are you a singer or something?'

'No. I mean, I was just curious to see how far it would carry in this distance. This space is pretty amazing.'

'Sounded a lot more desperate to me.'

'Desperate? Like how do you mean?'

'Terrified.'

'Terrified? No. Why would I be terrified? There's nothing around.'

'Like this,' Madilia said, and then let out an unearthly animal wail that had to have come directly from her ancestors. She jabbed the dun in the flanks and leaped out after her father. It was all Price could do to hold back his old gelding from joining the chase and leaving him dumped on the slope.

When he finally reached the bottom, Madilia and her massive father were nowhere in sight. His horse was twitchy and herd-bound now without the others and kept dancing in little circles with his ears pricked. The floor of the basin was deceptive. From their vantage point, high up on the grassy table, it had appeared to be fairly straightforward country, negotiable by spotting outcroppings or marooned cotton-woods in the distance and then simply tracking them point to point to maintain a true line of direction. Now that he was down in the bottom, though, his whole perspective changed. Dry riverbeds and cedar brakes that had seemed to be nothing more than narrow, twisting fissures from the high ground now turned into miniature Grand Canyons when confronted face-to-face. The walls of these chasms dropped straight down, maybe fifteen, twenty feet in most places, and then repeated themselves on the other side. A horseman had the option of either holding his nose and taking the blind plunge straight off the edge and hoping for the best or laboriously picking his way along the rims until he found a gentler descent. The third choice was to ride all the way around the brakes, zigzagging on the flat grassy ground while trying to maintain a visual objective in the distance that approximated a straight line. The problem for Price was that he had no clue what line to follow. Lowell and his daughter had completely vanished. There wasn't even a trace of dust, and no clear tracks were visible in the long grass. Price chose to hold his nose and take the leap. His old gelding was fearless and well accustomed to this kind of challenge, gathering his hocks up underneath him in short, firm strokes, then pricking his ears toward a landing point and catapulting straight toward the rocky bottom. When he landed, the horse was already in a full trot, legs churning for the opposite bank; then he grabbed hold with his front feet and lurched straight up the side like a bighorn sheep. When they arrived at the top, the horse shook himself all over and resumed his jagged trot as though he'd just gotten shed of a nasty fly.

Now Price was completely lost, and he knew it. He tried to locate the distant knob that Lowell had pointed out to him, but if he hadn't been sure of what he was looking at through the binoculars, now he was dumbfounded. He couldn't even spot the rim with the line of scrub pine. He twisted completely around in the saddle and stared at the overwhelming landscape. Crows glided out in a lazy line, squawking, then taking nosedives at one another. High above him, a hawk floated with its wings splayed out stiff, like giant arms. Price thought he could see its tiny head across the distance, jerking back and forth in search of some slight movement from earth. He waved his arms at the bird, but his horse got startled by this sudden movement and bolted. Price gathered up the reins and got him back to a nervous walk. He grabbed a shank of the black mane and ran it through his fingers, thinking this might bring him back around to some sense of the present and his lost predicament, but his attention was frazzled and edgy. He was shocked by the sight of his own hands. His knuckles seemed to be standing out, more prominent than usual. The broad fingernail on his index finger seemed even broader and the bulging callus beneath it. His hands became his father's hands, and he had to pry his eyes away, back to the sky, searching for the hanging hawk, but it had vanished. He kept hearing its shrill screech but couldn't spot it. The crows had landed off to his left and were fighting over the carcass of a young jackrabbit, playing tug-of-war with its intestines. He wanted to make sure this was taking place and reined his horse toward the flapping huddle, and when they flew off, cawing, he was satisfied. He stared down at the rabbit's dead head. A blue film cloaked its eyes, but the dark pupils were still staring out. As soon as he walked his horse on, the crows returned and started back up with their squabbling.

The rhythm of his horse's walk seemed to deepen the trance that Price felt himself falling into. He listened to the dull thud of the hooves and the way the sound changed when they entered tall grass. He heard the long tail switch at flies and the occasional snort as the horse cleared dust from his nostrils; the squeak of old leather. The whole presence of the horse startled him. The rolling motion of the shoulders and him up on top, the human passenger. Then he felt himself dissolve. He couldn't tell where the inside of his thighs left off and the saddle fenders began. The pulsing motion of his spine wasn't his own. It belonged to the horse. He was simply dumb cargo.

They creaked along to the brink of another gorge, and this time Price didn't even check the horse. He just grabbed mane and let him drop straight over the side into the unknown. He slacked the reins completely and allowed the bay to wander up the creekbed, slapping through rocks and picking gullies where the rain had cut deep black ruts. He thought if he wandered long enough, he'd get good and lost. He'd get so hopelessly lost that he'd be forced into some part of himself that he'd never known before. Some part he'd be forced to meet up with. The proposition thrilled and terrified him. It was the mind that wouldn't cooperate. He couldn't control the picturings. There was no rhyme or reason to their appearance. He watched them pop up in his head as though he were sitting in a Wednesday matinee from long ago, with no one else in the theater. He saw John Wayne wearing a buffalo coat. President Bush in a baseball cap, with a tie on. Bombs falling on Baghdad. Bombs seen from high above as though he were looking straight down through the hatch. The fat, self-satisfied face of General Schwarzkopf. A boy swinging a sledgehammer at the Berlin

Wall and not making a dent. Pictures of news. Pictures of faces making news. Pictures of crows and hawks. A dead rabbit's head. Then Madilia. Her eyes. Her violent, magnificent eyes.

7/91 (BELVIDERE, SOUTH DAKOTA)

The Package Man

The man in the suit was a smoking fool. He couldn't last thirty seconds between cigarettes. Even while he was smoking one, he was already fondling his wrinkled pack of Blue Trues on the bar, as though reassuring them that their time would come. He didn't once turn to Ray. Didn't even so much as cast a sideways peek at him. Ray peered down between his own knees to the splatters of calf blood on his boots. He rubbed the toe of each boot across the back of his ankles, but the blood remained. He didn't much care. He was beyond embarrassment where men in suits were concerned. He didn't know the guy from Adam anyhow.

'Cigarette?' the man piped up. Ray glanced over at him, but the man in the suit's eyes stayed fixed on the blue and white pack of cigarettes he held up in front of him. Ray wasn't even sure if the offer had been directed to him or if the guy was just blurting it out to himself in a drunken daze. Lots of loonies passed through this little town. It was ninety miles from nowhere, and the little yellow lights from the Hole in the Wall were like a magnet to the desperately road-weary.

'Thank ya, no,' Ray said. 'Got my own pack.'

'These I been smokin' for twenty-five years now. Blue Trues. Shoulda called 'em True Blues by now. That's a good long while to be faithful to any one brand in particular, don't you think? A good long while.'

'It is,' Ray agreed, and watched him now, but the man still didn't turn to meet his gaze. He jiggled the pack of Trues and watched the plastic filters rattle around against one another.

'Some guys like to skip around, but I'm more like the Canada goose.'

'What's that?' Ray said.

'Mated for life. Wolf's the same way, I understand. They say that about the wolf. Loon's another one. I find that pretty amazing.'

'Yeah,' Ray said, hoping to close the subject. The bartender slid Ray's drink toward him and asked if he'd like to see a menu. 'Yeah. Just throw a steak on and a baked potato.'

'That's my game,' the man in the suit persisted.

'What's that?'

'Beef. Meat.'

'I see.'

'Package man. That's my game. I'm a package man. Total carcass. We use it all.' Ray kept silent. The man started rapidly bouncing both his knees up and down and lit another cigarette while the first one still smoldered in the ashtray. 'Ground beef. Rib eyes. T-bones. Chops. Tender-loin. Entrails. Offal. We package the whole damn works.'

'That's something,' Ray muttered.

'Pays the rent. What's your game?'

'Me? I'm a hand. I'm just a hand.'

'Ah, bustin' yer ass on horseback! I know the feelin'. I'm from here.'

'You are?' Ray peered at him, thinking maybe he'd forgotten a face.

'Born and raised. Not a whole lotta future here, though. 'Less you think rubbin' yer butt raw on broncs is some kinda romantic way a life. I'm not talkin' about flying around in some Learjet and poppin' along the rodeo circuit. I'm talkin' about ranchin'. It's a piece a shit. I know about ranchin'.'

'Pays the rent,' Ray said to himself. The man reached down and snatched his attaché case off the floor, then slapped it down flat on the bar. He popped open the brass snaps and pulled out a small black computer, then hunched over it tensely, punching buttons and blowing smoke in little blue puffs. Ray thought maybe now the guy would leave him alone, but he kept right on, without straying from his computer figuring.

'You here for the fight last night?'

'No; I was out at the cow camp. I only get in town about once a week.'

'You missed a humdinger,' the man went on. 'One big slam-bang of a bar fight in here last night. You didn't hear about it?'

'No. I try to mind my own business.'

'Bar fight's anybody's business in a town this size. Source of inspiration. You got any idea how far it is to the nearest movie?'

'Yes, I do. It's about ninety miles.'

'You got that right. 'Less you wanna go up to Pierre and see some a that PG horseshit. I hate that crap. Parental Guidance! Who the hell are they kidding? The damn parents are children! You watch 'em. You see 'em line up for tickets. Bunch a damn teenagers. Can't wipe their own noses, let alone their children's. Babies having babies! Now, that's great for the future. That's gonna build some character and social fabric.'

Ray took a chug on his whiskey and swirled it around through the cracks in his teeth until it began to burn a little. He halfway considered walking out on his steak.

'You watch what happens in this country ten, fifteen years down the road. Sooner, maybe. Race a morons. Won't even be able to spell their own goddamn names. As it is now, they can't even keep their pants up. Parental Guidance, my ass.' The man went silent, as though a new thought had awakened some other part of himself. A part devoted to greed. He whipped out a pen and began jotting down figures on a napkin, copying them frantically off the tiny green screen of his computer. Ray watched his frenzied scrawl and smelled his steak coming at him through the kitchen door. 'Anyhow, you missed a hell of a brawl in here. They were bouncin' off the walls. Good old-fashioned fisticuffs. Lotta conflict in this little town. Always has been. On the outside it doesn't appear that way. Strangers roll through here, tourists. They think it's just a quaint, lazy little ranch community. What do they know? Lemme tell ya, there's conflict up the yin-yang here. You know that. Yer a cowboy.'

'Yeah,' Ray agreed, just to dull the moment.

'Like last night, for instance, it was supposed to be about selling beef to the military: air force and whatnot. That's part a my territory. I know somethin' about that. I've got firsthand experience. But this one guy claims he's not gettin' a fair shake from the government on account of he's half Lakota. Hell, he ain't even a full-blood, and he's complainin'. They get a damn check from the government and go out and burn it up on booze or sniff spray paint. Whose fault is that? They get free clothes, free housing, free medicine, and then bitch about the price a beef! Can you believe it? Anyhow, me, I ducked out the back emergency exit there. Complete chickenshit when it comes to violence. I don't know how you feel about it, but I'm just not crazy about pain. Suffering's another issue. I was born to suffer. We all were. That comes with the territory. But just out-and-out pain doesn't turn me on. How 'bout you? Are you a pain person?'

'What?' Ray said.

'Are you a seeker of pain? Maybe you are, being a hand and all that. Maybe you like that shit, but see, I'm not like that. I like the boiling hot tub full of frothy suds. The naked ladies. The good bottle of wine. A little TV, and it's beddy-bye for me. That's it. I'm not even a great craver of sex. I mean, it's okay. Sex is okay, don't get me wrong, but I'm not starved for it, like some. I don't hunt it down. I can rock and roll on my own. You know what I mean? I can watch. I can see the fabulous potential in a woman's body without having to actually possess it. In a way, it's more thrilling. The vision of it. The luscious tits and all that. I'm a big fan of that. Don't get me wrong. I just don't desperately need it, like some.'

Ray slammed back what was left of his Wild Turkey, slid off the stool, and headed for the men's room. The man in the suit never looked up. The green glow from the computer bounced off his eyes.

The bathroom had a split-pea-soup pallor to it, with pocketknife graffiti carved into the wooden molding and plaster: Indian insults. A joke about Nebraska Cornhuskers. Phone numbers for local blow jobs. Somebody's son was a faggot, and so was his old man. Ray didn't really feel compelled to take a leak; he'd just felt that his head might explode if he kept taking in the package man's ramblings. He had the sensation his head might actually blow right off his shoulders. All he'd heard for days was the bawling of calves; the snorting and farting of horses; hawks high above. He looked down at the dense yellow trickle of his own piss splashing off the wire mesh covering the drain. A soggy cigarette filter caught between the holes. The smell of Comet cleanser. The door popped open, and the package man pushed his way through, using his attaché case as a prod. 'Room for two in here?' He laughed, then pulled open the door to the toilet stall and let it slap closed behind him on a heavy spring. Ray said nothing. He didn't turn. He looked down and saw the man's shoes do an about-face beneath the stall panel. Ray hoped he wasn't going to proceed to take a dump, but then he saw the man's pants drop down around his ankles, and a little groan came from the stall, as though the effort to squat was slightly painful. 'Haven't been regular for three weeks now,' the man said as he lowered his butt to the seat. 'Comes from liquor, I suppose. Only drink when I'm on the road. Which is most the time. Back home it's off-limits. Wife just laid down the law one day, and that's how it's been ever since. Can't say I mind actually. Gives me a chance to dry out now and then. Body needs that, I think. Otherwise it starts to putrefy. End up smellin' just like your old man. That's the scary part. I hate that. Start feelin' like yer livin' out some doomed past. Some destiny you've got no say in. Women are good that way, doncha think? Keep us on the straight and narrow. I've got the kids too. They help. They're good that way too. Responsibility never hurt a man. I miss that when I'm out here in the field. Responsibility. Course, you gotta go where the beef is. That's the long and short of it. Can't sit behind a desk somewhere and dream out the window. Gotta go right to the source of it.' Ray didn't answer. He didn't bother washing his hands. He just zipped up and left the man sitting there.

His steak was waiting for him at the bar. As he slid back onto the stool and reached for the knife, he heard the shot hit the pea-green wall of the bathroom. It wasn't a loud shot, just a thudding bang like a firecracker makes. It wasn't even loud enough to draw the bartender's attention.

7/91 (KADOKA, SOUTH DAKOTA)

Synthetic Pink

(from *Edge of the World*)

Sometimes I see him. Sitting there. Content. Breaking his bread. Staring out the café window. Stirring his coffee in a dream. I can't tell what he's thinking, but it's not troubled. It's a calm face. No worries. His newspaper is folded neatly beside him; creased with precision. His glasses rest on the tablecloth. Everything is peaceful around him. Surrounded with order. He sips his soup in the European way, tipping the bowl and spooning away from himself. He wipes his upper lip meticulously with the linen napkin and then brushes the crumbs off his chin very gently. He returns the napkin to the same knee and spreads it smoothly, flicking away all the wrinkles. I see the ring on his little finger flashing. A liquid blue ring that sparkles from the sunlight through the window. A bird flits by outside, and his eyes rise to follow it, then return to the empty bowl of soup. He pushes the bowl to one side with both hands, then reaches slowly for the glass of water. He drinks and doesn't stop drinking until the glass is empty. I can see his throat throbbing as the icy water rushes through. His eyes close as though he's in an ecstasy and dreaming of something far away.

I was there when they opened his mouth and removed the dentures. They set his teeth on a stainless-steel table and attached a yellow tag with wire to them. The tag had numbers on it, written in black. The numbers were the date and time of his death. They attached another tag, with the same numbers, to the big toe of his right foot. Then they wheeled the body away. The yellow tag on his toe fluttered slightly, like a tiny flag, then disappeared through two swinging doors. The doors kept flapping for a while, then stopped. His teeth were left behind, all alone, on the stainless-steel table. The gums were synthetic pink, and there was still a piece of salad clinging between the molars. I turned the yellow tag over, and on the other side were more black numbers: his date of birth.

12/4/93 (NEW YORK CITY)

See You in My Dreams

She told me that she'd just had a phone call from a man called Esteban and that my father had been found dead in the little town of Bernalillo. Not actually found dead, because he'd died in the ambulance on the way to Albuquerque and lived long enough to identify himself; but dead in any case. Run over by a car.

The wind was still bashing the windows, and little clusters of rain would slap the glass, then subside. You could smell the accumulation of past fires through the moisture in the chimney. Fires long before we'd moved there.

I called Esteban, the little Mexican man who'd been looking out for my father for the past ten years. He was a tenant in the same dreary complex down off Conejo, and he'd taken a liking to my father, since they both spoke Spanish and shared a hard history with the bottle. His voice was genuinely heartbroken. I could hear him trying to control the quavering in it. He told me that a week ago, my dad had received some kind of big GI check in the mail from the government. A check he wasn't expecting. He'd gone out and cashed it; proceeded to get a military-style crew cut in the shopping mall; picked up a fishing license down at the gun shop, and took a cab all the way out to Pecos. Esteban tracked him there, because he was worried about all that money in the hands of a professional drunk. In Pecos he was afraid to approach him, because my dad was already on a rampaging binge. According to Esteban, he hooked up with a very large Indian woman named Matla, and they'd both gone upriver to trout-fish, with a bottle of gin. This was where Esteban lost them. He told me he was too much afraid of my father to tail him into the mountains where nobody was. He thought he might kill him.

Evidently, this Matla woman and my father spent three days fishing and drinking back in the Sangre de Cristo wilderness, then returned to Pecos and hired another cab to haul them all the way out to Bernalillo. By the time they hit town, Matla and the old man were not getting along. There were reports of out-and-out fistfights between them in the local bars. They were easy to remember: a very fat Apache woman with bare feet, and a tall, stringy white man with a red beard and a crew cut, both raging drunk. They careened their way from one end of town to the other, getting ousted from every bar until the money ran out. At that point, my dad staggered into the middle of the road and met his death.

The next morning I had to go down into town and sign some kind of official certificate, stating that I wished to have him cremated. Since the body was so badly mangled, that seemed the most appropriate procedure. They had all his personal articles lined up on a glass-topped desk, waiting for me to identify them: his wallet; his jackknife; his coins; his fishing license; and a strange iron-colored stone with a hole through the middle of it. They showed me a Xeroxed statement from the emergency medical team in Albuquerque, listing his blood alcohol level in red and, right next to it, the maximum legal level. He was way off the scale. There were other lists, detailing the various fractures, lesions, and traumas to the body. There were columns of numbers accounting for loss of blood and transfusions to replace it. Oxygen. Bandages. Splints. Neck braces. Swabs. Cotton. Injections. Everything detailing the nightmare of one lonely emergency, and below, in bold numbers, the total bill. They asked me to sign this paper and verify that I was the responsible party. As I took up the pen, the funeral manager began reciting all the options for burial containers, cemetery sites, and headstones. Since my dad had been an army air force pilot, I decided on the National Cemetery in Santa Fe and a plain pine box, about eight inches square, for his ashes.

That afternoon I went out and spent the day with Esteban, who was still very shaken. He fixed me some instant coffee with powdered creamer in a cup with a cracked handle. We sat in his little front room, facing a string of red chilies and a wooden crucifix hanging over the TV. Pictures of his son, calf-roping, hung on the walls, along with a calendar from the local feed store, advertising chicken mash. Esteban told me in a quiet voice how he'd had a premonition about my father's death. He'd seen it coming: 'I was a drinking man too, my friend. Oh, yes. I was very bad. Very, very bad. Many times I would tell this to your father, but he would never listen. You know how he was. He would listen to no one. I would bring him black bean soup to his door when I knew he'd not been eating for a week or more. I could tell when he was on one of his drunks. He would never come outside, and you could hear him singing in Spanish all night. Loud singing. I would bring him the hot soup, and he would see me coming through his window and start to yell at me like a dog. He would yell that he needed no food. Food was for the living! he'd yell. He'd call me all kinds of bad names; Mexican names. And then he'd throw things at me, like his boots or beer cans. So I would just leave the bowl of soup by his door, but then he would come out and kick it into the yard. Sometimes he would try to chase me, but he always fell. If I tried to help him up he would curse me in the worst Spanish, call me cabrón and things like that. I knew it was the booze causing this devil in him, so I never could take it personally, although it hurt my feelings sometimes. I would try to remember all the quiet times we had. Sober. Sitting by his front door just listening to coyotes or faraway voices. He had a good mind, your father. Muy listo.' Esteban's eyes had a bluish-gray cast to them, like the kind of eyes that are slowly going blind from cataracts. He wept for my father, silently, and bent slowly forward in his chair, clasping his stomach with both hands. I reached over to him and touched his knee. He nodded his head and expelled a short blast of grief. It sounded like a child moaning in sleep. 'I will miss him,' he said. 'It's difficult to make a friend. Hacerse amigos. Muy dificil. But we had good times. We laugh. We sing along sometimes to the Border Radio stations. Your father loved the music. We sometimes argued about stupid things. About Willie Nelson. He was mad that Willie Nelson made so much money off the old songs from your father's childhood. Like "Moonlight in Vermont" and another one – "Georgia," that was it. He was mad about this, but I told him if it makes people happy to hear these things, then why be angry. But then his mind would lock down. He would get that terrible anger in his face, and he would say that it was a matter of honor. Certain things should remain as they were. Sagrado, you know. Cherished, I think he said. That was the word he used. Cherished. And then it was as though he, alone, was left on earth to defend these things. Moralmente obligado. And I would have to slowly talk him out of it. Talk him through the other side of his anger until he began to breathe again like a human man. And we would share our can of Coca-Cola and he would roll his cigarettes and line them up on the sidewalk in front of us. And soon a laugh would come. Over nothing. Just a word or a thought. Then things would be all right for a while. Things would be fine between us.' Esteban paused and asked me if I wanted some more instant coffee and then apologized for it being instant. 'Real coffee is very high right now.' I agreed, and we sat in silence for a while. Esteban rocked gently in his chair, then laughed with an old memory. 'One other time, I can remember an argument we had. This was funny. It was about the word "Chicano." Your father refused to use this word. He said he'd been calling my people "Mexicans" all his life, and after all this time, how was it supposed to come out "Chicano"? He asked me what it meant and I told him "Mexican American" and he said this was too confusing. It was invented by politicians or something, just to confuse people and set them apart. He refused to use it. He called me "paisano," which was fine by me. I called him the same in return. We were good friends.'

Esteban walked me over, across the concrete courtyard, to my father's one-room apartment and left me there on a weedy patch of grass, facing his door. He touched my shoulder very softly and walked away. I just stood there for a while, afraid to go in. The same fear that invaded me at his door when he was alive. The very same fear. There was a sign nailed to his door, saying *Mad Dog* in red letters, with a cartoon face of a snarling bulldog, foaming at the mouth. Hanging from the green fiberglass awning were long chains made from aluminum pop-off tabs of beer cans, all linked together and tinkling in the desert breeze. I threaded my way through the chains and opened the door. I couldn't understand my pounding fear as I entered the dark room. My whole body was throbbing with it, as though he were still there; still sitting in the broken-down rocker that I'd bought him years before; still hunkered over his ready rolls, surrounded by stacks of magazines and papers and his black radio propped on an orange crate, squawking Mexican polkas. I parted the plastic curtains and the sun poured onto the walls, collaged with pictures torn from magazines and Scotch-taped to the plaster: Bing Crosby with a pipe; Loretta Lynn; Dolly Parton; English setters galloping across an ocean of emerald lawn; Hank Williams's tombstone; burros carrying loads of pottery and firewood; nocturnal frogs with yellow eyes clinging to jungle trees; curled-up photos of me and my sisters in our 4-H uniforms, showing sheep at the county fair. On the little table in front of the rocker were opened cans of half-eaten tuna fish and a crusty bowl of Esteban's black bean soup. Stacks of *National Geographic*, *Look*, and *Life*, all barricading the table, with a narrow alleyway leading out toward the sink. A peanut butter jar on the floor, half filled with brown water and soggy cigarette butts. Piles of letters he'd written and never sent. One to me, which he ended by saying: 'You may think this great calamity that happened, way back when – this so-called disaster between me and your mother – you might actually think that it had something to do with you, but you're dead wrong. Whatever took place between me and her was strictly personal. See you in my dreams.'

My aunt and uncle and my two sisters arrived at the house the next day. We sat in front of the fireplace, and my uncle Buzz told stories of him and my dad growing up on the Illinois farm in McHenry, with their five brothers. Stories of how my dad was always wandering off when he was little and getting lost in the acres of tall corn. He'd wind up on some neighboring farm with his dog, Gyp, and have to spend the night there until my grandfather could come get him. Stories of how they'd secretly climb up into the hayloft to get a view of the draft mares getting bred, because my grandfather had strictly forbidden children from being present. 'There was this old boy, Wilters I think his name was, and he had one of those mammoth jack mules – you know, with the dorsal stripe down the spine – big huge son of a buck. And anyway, old Wilters had himself a regular traveling stud service with this mule for all the farmers in the county. He'd get himself all duded out with a derby hat and a black suit come spring, and he'd tether that mule to the hind bumper of his Model T and just drive around from farm to farm, servicing any mare that could stand it. I remember me and your dad looking down and watching that – we must've been about eight or nine years old. Boy, I'll tell you, that was something. Our first real vision of the "deed," you know. And then old Wilters, he'd take off his derby after the mare was settled, and he'd hold it out to your grandpa, and he'd drop five bucks in the hat, and Wilters would slap the derby back up on his head with the five bucks in it. Then they'd all crack a bottle and pass it around and talk about crops and grain prices. We'd have to hold our breath sometimes to keep from sneezing, up in all that hay, and getting found out. But we'd just stay up there until Wilters finally drove off, with his old mule trotting along behind that Model T.'

We stayed in front of the fireplace for a long time, and, slowly, my uncle began to stretch out and smile. His stories became like small links for me in the mystery of my father: 'Your grandpa was the drinker, though. Oh, brother, could he put away the muscatel. I told you about when I was coming down Columbine that one afternoon and saw that smoke pouring out of the second-story window. Out his bedroom window. Smoke just billowing out into the elm trees. I go charging into the house and up the stairs, and there he is, out cold on the bed, and the whole mattress is on fire. He's just laying there in a stupor. So I scoop him up in my arms – by that time, you know, he only weighed about ninety pounds; he'd pretty much wasted away – and I carry him down and set him on the couch, then I go running back up there and grab the mattress and heave it out the window, onto the lawn. Well, about that time, your grandma comes home from church and I'm out there on the lawn with the hose, soaking the mattress, and she comes striding over – you know how she was – she comes over to me and wants to know why in hell I'm ruining a perfectly good mattress. I say, Ma, it's burned clear through – there's a hole this big in the damn thing – and besides that, I saved her husband. Well, she didn't want to know anything about him. All she cared about was that mattress. I said to her, Ma, I saved Dad! I just saved him! He was about to burn up alive! And she just gave that little snort she always did and strode off. That was her, all right.'

We all got dressed up the next morning and drove out to the National Cemetery, following the long winding path through acres of marble military crosses, all the same, each one festooned with a little American flag. Vietnam. World War II. Korea. Like fields of corn rows, planted in sweeping curves. I had asked for one of those upright marble crosses for his headstone, but they told me they'd run out, as a consequence of Vietnam. So I settled for a little white slab, set flat in the ground, engraved with his name, rank, and the dates of his life. There was a green canvas awning, with benches and folding chairs set up on a hill for the service. It wasn't raining, and the awning cast a greenish tint on everyone's face. There was a larger gathering than I'd expected. Mostly alcoholics or ex-alcoholics. You could see it in their ravaged faces. Then just some people from the housing complex who'd known my dad one way or the other. Simple people. Many of them stood with their hands crossed in front of their waists, as though embarrassed to take a seat; eyes on the ground. I didn't recognize any of them, except for Esteban, who smiled at me, then lowered his head.

Me and my younger sister took turns reading some Lorca poems (my dad's favorite poet), and I even attempted a passage from the Bible but choked on the words 'All is vanity,' because I suddenly saw my own in reading this as though I understood its true meaning. I couldn't speak at all for a while. Nothing came out. My whole face quivered, and I could sense the embarrassment from the gathering. I felt no embarrassment myself, only a terrible knotted grief that couldn't find expression. I stood there, waiting for it to pass, but it didn't. It held me there for what seemed like a very long time, until finally it dissolved enough to allow me to finish. I read the rest of the passage without emotion and with no connection to any of the words. I was just grateful to get through it.

The funeral director got up in front, with his gray suit and dark glasses, a total stranger who looked more like a CIA agent than a mediator for the dead. He read off the standard military funeral sermon from the U.S. Government. The same sermon read before every cross in this cemetery: '… in deep gratitude for services rendered in the line of duty …' Then he presented me with an American flag, folded in the traditional triangle, and shook my hand. I shook everyone's hand that day and embraced people I didn't know.

As we were all leaving, I turned back toward the canvas awning and saw the little pine box with the ashes, sitting on the fold-out table; just sitting there with no one around. I felt pulled back toward it as if by gravity; as though there were still something left unfinished in this ceremony. Off to the side were two Chicano men, squatting by a yellow backhoe in front of the open grave. They were waiting until everyone cleared out, so they could put the box in the hole and cover it up. As I walked back toward them, they turned their heads and stared into the grave, trying not to look me in the eye. I picked up the pine box, surprised by how much it weighed. Just ashes from a dead man. The gravediggers turned their backs toward me and lowered their heads. I was grateful to them for that.

3/89 (LOS ANGELES)

Southwest
Chief

Mrs. Ortega is trying to put her little girl to bed in roomette number 6, right across the aisle from me. She's wearing a black leather skirt with gold spiked high heels, and chunks of turquoise mounted in silver clanking around her neck. Now and then her jewelry knocks the little girl in the forehead, but she doesn't make a sound. She sits straight up in the bunk bed while her mother tucks the blankets around her. She's staring out at Barstow as it flashes by the window in the night; Portland cement trucks working under peach-colored spotlights in the pits below the tracks. Storage warehouses fly by. Grim little Sheetrock neighborhoods dissolve into white sand, then reappear and dissolve again. Mrs. Ortega's little girl asks her mother about Rafael: 'Adónde está Rafael?' And her mother answers, 'No se,' while her Navajo concho belt slaps against the glass door.

The Southwest Chief comes grinding into old Barstow station, one of the last Spanish-style stations left on the

Santa Fe Trail. Now its windows are all smashed out, framed by dark brick and fractured stucco. Dried pigeon shit drips across the words *Casa del Desierto* carved into a bleached-out wall. Ghosts of redcaps long gone hunch into the night, still pushing their iron-wheeled wagons loaded high with lizard luggage for the rich barons of the Citrus Empire. 'What's that?' Mrs. Ortega's little girl wants to know. 'Nothing. Go to sleep now.'

'Is that Rafael!' she squeals, coming out of her blue blankets.

'No. Rafael is gone. Now you must go to sleep.'

I head for the lounge, squeezing past Mrs. Ortega's large leather rump. Her little girl is still sitting straight up; still hunting the darkness outside for any sign of Rafael. The train lurches on as I make my way up the narrow aisle. Giant concrete towers float by in the darkness, blinking their warnings to aircraft. An old gray couple stop dead in their tracks as they see me approach. They are both severely bent over at the waist and use aluminum canes. They have no idea how to negotiate around me in all the swaying, so I duck into an empty sleeper, with the door wide open, to let them pass. We repeat 'Excuse me' a few times as they go reeling by like drunken dancers. As they pass, I can tell they're from the country by the way the old woman grabs onto the belt loops of her husband's jeans.

In the nonsmoking lounge, zombies are staring blankly at a sitcom on TV sets mounted high in the dark corners of the car. All the sets are tuned to the same channel. Nobody's laughing. Nobody's talking. Just the canned laughter from the TVs and the corny one-liners. I descend into the smoking lounge, which is thick with smoke and talking people, and order a gin and tonic in a white plastic cup. Three girls with tattoos all over their arms are smoking up a storm and talking about drapes and carpeting. One of them has a great laugh. One of those laughs that go out of control, and you know she's not worried about what people think. I sit in a corner where I can watch the whole room. I'm ready to watch. I've been working with detectives lately, and the whole idea of watching has begun to fascinate me. I dissolve into this corner and go into my 'detective eyes.' That's what I'm working on right now: how to watch without being seen. You have to be careful, because if people see you watching them they immediately change into something else; something they weren't the moment before. They become suspicious and want to hide, or hostile and want to kill you. You've got to watch your step. A huge woman in green approaches and wonders if I'd mind if she sits down right across the table from me. She wants to rest her bones, she says. She has a face that's seen a lot of road. Eyes that look beat up by booze and endless nights. Her name is Rose, from Albuquerque, and it turns out both her parents are buried in the National Cemetery at Santa Fe; same place my dad is buried. Me and Rose have death in common. She's just returning from visiting family up near Pendleton, Oregon, and tells me about the orange moon rising over the snowcapped peaks; coveys of quail under the pine trees; and the ingenious heating system in her relative's house, all solar conducted. Rose was raised in Albuquerque, and she's heading back. She says she doesn't know where else to go. She's tried all kinds of places but always ends up coming black. 'I guess it's hard to git rid of where you're from.' A black guy with an L.A. Raiders cap is talking louder than anyone to a mean-looking kid in a leather jacket. He goes on about some 'Italian bitch' with a huge rock on her finger who lived in a real quiet neighborhood somewhere. How bad he wants to get back there and see her; take up where he left off. He's living for that. Rose runs out of things to say. She hoists herself up from the table with her elbows, pulling the green rayon sweater down around her gigantic hips. 'Maybe I'll see you up at the cemetery sometime,' she says, and raises her glass in parting. 'Maybe.'

The tattoo girls are having a great time. They're self-contained, flying by train through the night, heading toward the Painted Desert. They've got companions to see them through. Their camaraderie excites them. Me, I'm glad I'm alone. Watching. I drift back to the detectives' conference room in the Wilshire precinct. Each in his own little cubbyhole, reviewing cases. The grisly cases. The stabbed, mauled, burned, shot up, mutilated, strangled, of L.A. I like working with detectives. They all seem like lonely men to me. I don't know if it's the job that makes them that way or if lonely men are attracted to the job. I'm flying by train.

2/2/89 (LOS ANGELES TO CHICAGO)

Falling
Without
End

I'm an actor now; I confess. I don't fly. I've been having some trouble landing jobs lately because of this not wanting to fly business; plus, I refuse to live in L.A. I live as far away from L.A. as possible. In the South. Not the Deep South but South enough where they still call a river a 'ribah' and a Buick a 'Brewick.' I don't own a fax machine or an answering service or call forwarding or a cellular car phone or a word processor, and I've never volunteered for what they call 'press junkets.' I'm not sure where the term 'junket' came from in relation to the press, but I never did like the sound of it very much. It has a military ring to it, or maybe tapioca pudding; I'm not sure which. On top of all this, I'm not getting any younger and my face is falling apart. Most of my lower teeth were knocked out by a yearling colt in the spring of '75. Half my upper teeth are badly discolored, and one of them's been dead for as long as I can remember.

When you get right down to it, I'm lucky to even have an agent at this point in time.

I've been involved in many dangerous, foolish things over the years. More by accident than choice. I've been upside down under falling horses at a full gallop. I've been fired upon by a twelve-gauge Ithaca over-and-under. I've rolled in a 1949 Plymouth coupe, which is a hard car to flip over; and I almost blew myself up once with a plastic milk bottle full of white gas on the Bay of Fundy, where they have the highest tides in the world. Still, I would gladly go through all these dumb acts ten times over rather than get on an airplane of any kind. I admit to an overwhelming vertigo that I don't quite understand and I'm unwilling to psycho-analyze. Suffice it to say, it's a severe problem of the imagination. The inability to control mental picturings of stupefying height; and the ensuing sensations associated with these picturings. The absolutely realistic sensation of falling without end, for instance. That's one I have no power over. In any case, luckily I love to drive. I've learned to love to drive. I love long-distance driving. The farther the better. I love covering immense stretches in one leap: Memphis to New York City; Gallup to L.A.; Saint Paul to Richmond; Lexington to Baton Rouge; Bismarck to Cody. Leaps like these. Without a partner. Completely alone. Relentless driving. Driving until the body disappears, the legs fall off, the eyes bleed, the hands go numb, the mind shuts down, and then, suddenly, something new begins to appear.

2/25/90 (CHARLESTON, WEST VIRGINIA)

The Hero
is in
His Kitchen

Hey, John? It's Clayton.

Who?

Clay.

Say it again.

Clayton Miles.

You don't sound like him.

Well, it's been a while.

It has been that. Great day! How long's it been?

I haven't kept track.

Where are you now?

Arizona. Somewhere outside Tucson. I'm in a Texaco phone booth.

Well, I'm in bed.

It's daytime there, isn't it?

Far as I can tell.

Are you sick or something?

Nope. Just no reason to get up. I'm conducting all my business from here. It's perfect. Angel just made me a vodka tonic, and I'm working on my tapes.

Which tapes?

Well, right now I'm working on my soundtrack tapes from famous chase scenes. You remember *Bullit*? Steve McQueen? Just finished that one. Here, listen to this. I'll play it for you.

John! Hey, Johnny! I'm in a pay phone here, and I haven't got much change!

What's the matter?

I'm low on change.

I thought you were a movie star now. How come you're low on change?

Just haven't got a lot on me.

What're you doing in Tucson? Playing cowboys and Indians again?

Just going through on my way to L.A. I wanted to talk to you for a second.

Good. Maybe we could meet up when you get down there.

That'd be great, but I've gotta meet Irene there too. She's coming.

How come she's not with you?

We're going through a bad spell.

Aw, that's too bad. I hate those. Just went through one of those myself.

You did?

Yep.

Well, that's kinda what I wanted to talk to you about.

Yeah. Just got over it, in fact. Pure torture. That's why I'm still in bed. Wiped out from it.

Yeah.

Thought I was dying there for a while. I'd just collapse and pray for death.

But Angel's with you, right?

Yeah. Angel's right here. She just made me a tall vodka tonic with a twist of lime. Rose is here too.

They're both there?

Yep.

How's that working out?

It has its ups and downs. Like I said, we just went through a little slump, but we're back on top of it now. They're best friends again. Oh, that reminds me! I had this thought before, and I've been trying to remember what it was, and just now something about what you said reminded me of it. Maybe that's the reason you called.

Maybe what's the reason?

In order to remind me of this thought.

Yeah, maybe. But what I really wanted to talk about was Irene.

Good. Let me just tell you this before I forget it again. I don't want to lose this.

Okay. Just a second. I gotta drop more quarters in.

Go ahead.

All right. You still there? John?

Yeah. You can always count on me, pal. But listen – this is it. I've just gone through this whole jealousy thing with Angel. I mean *her* jealousy, not mine. We were just coming through the worst part of it, and I thought maybe I should give her a line that was a great Sterling Hayden kind of line. Maybe that would work, I thought. So I said to her, I said, 'If you loved me you'd be blind to all my faults.' That's what I said. And just as I said that I caught myself trying to *be* Sterling Hayden. I could have just as easily said it from myself, but what I saw behind it was this real basic feeling that I'm not good enough as I am; that I would be better off being somebody else. Like Sterling Hayden, for instance. And then, when I saw that, at the same time I realized that this was all in my thoughts, all in my head, but in actual fact I *am* Sterling Hayden.

John, listen – I'm running out of change.

No, look – I don't mean that I think I'm Sterling Hayden. That's not it. What I'm saying is that I actually *am* the person in my daydreams. No matter who it is. Harry Truman, Walter Winchell – it doesn't matter. The fact is that I'm actually here, and this adventure is mine. The pretending is all part of it. You see what I mean?

Yeah, but look –

The other way, it's like not seeing the movie that you're in. Thinking you're not in a similar situation to the movie. Wishing all the time for something that's already taking place. But the hero lays in bed with the girl just exactly like me and Angel are now.

You're both in bed now?

Yeah, sure. All three of us. Rose is here too. You wanna say hi to her?

No. Look – maybe I should try you some other time.

No – are you kidding! No time like the present! But look – what I'm trying to say is, you're watching this scene in the movie, the guy and girl in bed. You've seen it a million times, in a million different movies. They're at her place and it's dark and they're dreaming out through the cloudy windows and he's smoking a Camel. You've paid your five bucks and you're sitting there with your popcorn watching this scene and you say, 'God, I wish I had that! I wish my life was like that!' But what you're not realizing is that your ordinary, everyday life *is* that. I'm not talking about playing a part. I'll leave that up to you actors. I'm saying that the part that you're actually living is just like the one you're playing.

Yeah, right. Okay. I just thought maybe I could ask you for a little advice –

I mean I *am* that guy laying in the dark with the beautiful girl, looking out the cloudy window, smoking a Camel and drinking a vodka tonic. I am that guy right now. That's me.

That's great.

But I don't ordinarily recognize it. I keep yearning for what I already have. But now, suddenly, a possibility opens up! A new light! I suddenly see my life as a real adventure. I actually experience it in that way you experience a movie. The sound track surrounds me! I'm in it!

Look, John –

Even an ordinary scene, where the hero is in his kitchen, frying eggs, and the camera's tracking in very slowly, and there's spooky music in the background, which supposedly the hero can't hear, only the audience can hear it – but basically, he's just there in his kitchen doing something very banal like frying a couple eggs. And you're there in the audience, transfixed by this situation, and yet you never have that kind of feeling when you're in your own kitchen frying your own eggs. You see what I mean? We're actually the heroes of our own kitchens, Clay! Do you realize that? We are the heroes of our very own kitchen!

I've run out of quarters, John. I'm gonna have to call you when I get to L.A.

You're on the road again! Well, lackaday! It was good hearing you, Clayton old man.

You too.

Don't buckle under the weight of a heavy heart! That's my advice to you. Never surrender!

Adiós.

3/18/90 (TUCSON, ARIZONA)

Homage
to Céline

I have an appointment this morning with the costume and makeup departments of a German production company at a tacky hotel on Highland. It's a favorite of the heavy metal bands, for some reason, and their groupies are crawling all over the lobby and hovering around the elevator for any sign of their heroes. I share the elevator up with about six of these bimbos, who are all using the same plastic makeup kit, painting their eyelids with some kind of peach-colored glitter cream, and then pinching their tiny nipples to make them stand out erect. They're not giggling or seeming to have a good time, like chicks in the fifties. Their anticipation seems completely pent up inside a burning desire to be absolute victims.

I find the room on the thirtieth floor, and as soon as I enter and see the racks of costumes hanging and the faces of people I'll be related to for the next four months, all of us strangers thrown together in this desperate effort to put images on film, my heart just sinks. I want to either run or puke, but it's too late for either.

The small Italian tailor, dressed very smartly in a blue pin-striped suit, is arguing intensely with the German costume designer, a huge Valkyrie of a woman in a Mexican serape and silver-tipped cowboy boots. She towers above the tailor and smokes like a dragon, drawing the exhale from her mouth up into her nostrils with long, delicious pulls, causing the smoke to hover like a fog all around her upper lip. She's upset about the fabric the tailor has chosen. It's too soft and contemporary, in her opinion. 'This is a fifties movie!' she proclaims. 'They didn't have these fabrics in the fifties! They were never even invented back then.' The Italian man shrugs and snorts and turns his back on her, pulling his long yellow tape measure back and forth across the back of his neck as though trying to saw his head off with it.

The makeup man comes over and wants to try several varying shades of gray in my hair for the aging sequences; about a dozen varieties of flesh tones for the face; and he's very excited about experimenting with some fake blood. 'His wounds are unique,' he says. 'They must be absolutely unique.'

An assistant to the costume designer keeps shoving expensive pairs of handmade English shoes at me, all designed specifically for the period. Boxes of period watches, period rings, cuff links, fountain pens, handkerchiefs, reading glasses, cigarette cases, tie clasps, and belts are displayed on a card table, awaiting my preference. The room is very hot and stuffy, and somebody opens a window, allowing some of the dragon lady's smoke to escape. Coffee tables are littered with half-eaten glazed doughnuts and grungy Styrofoam cups; ash-trays heaped with butts. The phone is continually ringing, and the person being called is never the one who answers. About four different languages are going on simultaneously.

The assistants to the director are going over my travel arrangements from L.A. to the Mexican border at Laredo. They say that because of Mexican regulations, they can't get an American rental car company to risk letting one of their cars across the border, so they're trying to hire two Mexican drivers from Mexico City to bring their own limo up and then drive me back down to Veracruz. They chuckle to each other slyly, and one of them says: 'Of course, the whole thing would be a lot easier on all of us if you flew.'

'I don't,' I say.

'Yes, we know.' Throughout all this the tiny Italian tailor is weaving in and out around my body, taking measurements and whispering numbers to an assistant, who jots them down in a notepad. (Everyone seems to have an assistant on this deal.)

The director himself comes in and asks if I would mind reading with three actresses he's auditioning for the small role of my girlfriend. He wants to videotape the auditions in a separate room, so I follow him down there. All three of these actresses are waiting nervously in the hallway, twisting their scripts in their hands and wetting their lips. The German director can't find the key to this room, so he leaves me there in the hallway with the three nervous girls while he goes off to find the key. I can't stand being smiled at by these three young hopefuls, so I excuse myself and pretend I'm going to look for a drinking fountain. I slip into the elevator, and there're two rockers slumped in a corner, dressed in black leather and aluminum armbands. They look entirely pissed off about everything in general.

As I bail out into the lobby, two more assistants to the director rush up to me and say they've run into even more snags with the limo proceedings. 'I don't need a limo,' I tell them.

'No, we'll get you a limo; don't worry about that. It's just that they have the same problem at the border as we do.'

'What problem's that?' I say.

'Insurance. They're afraid their car will be stolen or resold, and they don't want to take the risk.'

'I don't need a limo. Just get me a Chevy.'

'Same problem with a Chevy.'

'Get me a Ford, then.'

'It doesn't matter what kind of car it is. They're just not willing to risk it.' The other assistant chimes in, with a big shit-eating grin: 'There's really no problem with the limo. I mean, the only real problem is paying off the federales. It's essentially the same problem that an American limo service would have. Just a little less expensive.'

'Just get me a Chevy,' I repeat.

'We'll work it out. Don't worry. We'll have everything set up by the time you're ready to go. Sure would be easier if you flew, though.' The two of them rush off toward the elevator with their loose-leaf notebooks, beepers, and head-sets. I hit Highland and walk. I love walking in a town where nobody else does. The sidewalks are like the desert.

Back at my hotel, Secret Service men are swarming all over the parking lot and entrance. You can tell they're Secret Service men because they all wear the same kind of business suit and have the same severe haircuts, and they all have these little flesh-colored plastic ear microphones, which they believe are invisible to the public at large. They're milling around with darting eyes and appear to be madly talking to themselves, when in fact they're whispering to one another through their little devices.

There's a note for me at the concierge desk: 'Sorry about the missing key. I finally found it. We missed you but went ahead with the audition anyway. I believe we've found someone really wonderful.' Signed, the director.

'Is there a diplomat in the house?' I ask the uniformed desk clerk.

'Excuse me?' he says, twitching his eye, and his face goes into a masked smile as though he were selling Pepsodent.

'A politician? There's all those goons outside.'

'Oh, I see. Yes, sir. We have visitors from the Middle East.'

'Anyone I know?'

'I'm sorry, sir, but we're not allowed to give out any kind of information.'

'I get ya.' I give him a clandestine wink, which baffles him completely.

Upstairs, in the hallway right across from my room, are stacks of room-service trays, dozens of them, all smashed up against the walls. Every tray is loaded with the remains of fancy desserts. Key lime pie, chocolate mousse, crème brûlée – nothing but desserts; all half eaten, nibbled on and squashed together; oozing over the edges onto the plush-flowered carpet. I see a dark arm, draped in a white tunic with gold embroidery, emerge from the doorway across from my room, extending yet another tray brimming with dessert garbage. The arm sets the tray down on top of the nearest stack, then a face peeps out of the doorway and stares at me. It's a scared little face, with black, beady eyes and a short goatee. As soon as the face sees me it darts back into the room like a groundhog and bolts the little chain latch inside. I can hear him chattering nervously to two other men, behind the closed door. It sounds like Arabic. The door pops open again, to the limit of the chain, and a pair of dark glasses stares out at me. The door slams shut, and there's more nervous chatter. Just as I get my door unlocked, a room-service wagon comes around the corner, pushed by a blond kid in a uniform like the Philip Morris man's. The wagon is loaded with desserts and headed my way. I duck inside and find myself frantically latching the chain to my door and turning the dead bolt. Fear is contagious.

Inside my room, I can't move for a while. I don't know why. It's not fear now; it's something else. I just stand there, staring at the carpet. Nothing in me wants to move. I have no idea when or if I'll ever move again. I wait for something to start up; some slight motivation. I want to see what it is that finally propels me into action. Nothing comes. *I could stand here through the night*, I'm thinking. *I could maybe stand right here till morning. Someone would find me. Room service would find me. The maid. Someone would wonder why there's no response in this room. No answer to the door. The telephone.* The phone begins to ring, as though my thought caused it to go off. I stand right there. The phone continues; three, four, five rings, and they give up. Whoever it was. *Probably more horseshit about the limo. What if someone's died, though? It could've been that. Some emergency. Who would die? Who would die now? It could be any one of us. I'll find out later. If it's that, they'll leave a message at the desk.* I check the message service. Nothing. I'm in motion now without seeing it; without having caught the moment. That's how it is. Sleep-walking, more or less. A trance of some kind. I pace the room. There's not much to walk. I go through all the products displayed on the marble counter beside the sink. They've thought of just about everything: collapsible tooth-brush, shoeshine kit, shower cap, deodorant, conditioner, aftershave lotion, shampoo, mouthwash, hair blower, three kinds of soap in three different colors with three different smells, even a little sewing kit. There's a white terry-cloth robe with the logo of the hotel embroidered on the pocket in blue. There's a note in the sash stating that this robe can be purchased at the front desk if so desired, but the guest is welcome to use it free of charge. In other words, don't steal it. I strip down and put it on. I don't know why I'm doing this. I never wear bathrobes. I wander around in this bulky robe and a silly pair of matching shower slippers. I prowl the room. I crack a miniature bottle of gin out of the minibar and drink it straight down. I cruise the room some more. There's impressionistic Monet-type lithographs of water lilies on all the walls in pastel colors. There's a magazine on the glass table with a head shot of Michelle Pfeiffer and her juicy lips. A room-service menu on the side table, next to some white mints. I stare at the list of desserts. The phone rings again. I answer it automatically. It's those pesky assistants to the director, on a conference line, with more frantic information about Mexico. The latest is that the limo owned by the two Mexican drivers has a lien on it, and they won't allow the car to cross the border; so now they've arranged for an American driver (actually he turns out to be Austrian) to take me by Lincoln Town Car from L.A. down to Laredo, where I'll be met by the Mexicans in a Chevy Century, and they'll drive me the rest of the way down to Veracruz. 'A Lincoln Town Car? What's a Lincoln Town Car?' I say.

'A stretch limo!' they say in unison, full of enthusiasm. 'It's very beautiful. It's midnight blue!'

'I told you I didn't need a limo.'

'Yes, but we've got you a Chevy at the border. So now you have both.'

'Fine,' I say. 'That's just fine.' I hang up and move out on the balcony with more miniature gin and my terry-cloth robe. The tall palm trees aren't moving at all now, and there's not a ripple in the pool. *Murder weather*, I'm thinking. This is the perfect weather to kill someone in. *If someone had nothing better to do, this is the weather that would cause him to think about maybe killing. Maybe just dogs. Going around through every backyard in the neighborhood and killing dogs. Maybe just that.*

Down below, on the street bordering the parking lot, there's a long line of motorcycle cops, their bikes parked and the front wheels all tilted in the same direction, like a frozen parade. The cops stand around in a group with their legs wide apart and their arms crossed on their chests; they grin and crack jokes behind amber dark glasses. Two black stretch limos are stationed right in front of the lobby doors, with their trunks wide open. (What is this thing about limos and luxury? Limos and luxury. Limos and luxury. It's a trick on mortals. Why can't they just give me a Chevy.) Now the Secret Service goons are buzzing around the black limos, loading dozens of leather attaché cases into the trunks. All of these attaché cases have combination locks, and they're hooked together through the handles with silver cable and then padlocked. There're so many attaché cases that the doorman can't get the trunk shut on one of the cars. A Secret Service man rushes over and shoves the doorman out of the way, rearranges the attaché cases, then slams the trunk shut and locks it. He glares at the doorman as he shoves the car key in his pocket. The doorman's feelings are hurt. You can tell even at the distance I'm watching from that his feelings are hurt. His whole body declares it. He's wearing one of those ridiculous outfits with the funny cap and gold lapels. A throwback to the era of a ruling-class mentality that won't lay down and die. He rubs his patent-leather shoe on the back of his pant leg and tries to regain his composure. He tries to act like a good servant. Suddenly, from out of the revolving door of the lobby comes the little dessert fanatic who inhabits the room right across from mine. I recognize him by his white embroidered tunic and his little goatee. On either side of him is a burly bodyguard with a firm grip on his elbow. The back door of the closest limo flies open, and the little guy is whisked into the car. The door slams shut and the engine fires almost simultaneously. All the motorcycle cops mount up in unison and crank their Harleys. The whole long phalanx moves out into the street, with traffic being stopped in every direction. I'm sure glad I'm not in politics.

I move back into the room, and the same sensation hits me as before. I come to a dead stop. The miniature gin slips from my hand. I stare at the blank screen of the TV set. Surrounded by luxury. A luxury that can't come anywhere near touching this emptiness. A voice next door. An urgent, persuasive voice on the phone. Pacing. A business deal of some kind. Movies. Something to do with the movies. I'm still not moving. The sound of cars down below taking off from a traffic light; all of them at once, as though they've just been released. Moving toward the mountains. Music. Somebody's radio. Marvin Gaye. It's his voice. 'Sexual Healing.' Murder again. Why murder? Shot in the head by his dad. Shot dead in the head. Why murder?

I'm moving again, without knowing how. Without seeing. Back to the bathroom. Back to the products. I stare at myself in the mirror, but I recognize that I don't stare at myself in the same way I did when I was sixteen. I'm not looking for the same things anymore. I'm simply in a state of shock. I can see that in my eyes now. Like a horse on painkiller. Bute or Ace. Just numb.

I take off this dumb white robe and change into something that I hope they'll allow me into the lounge with. I'm heading down to the bar. Now I've got a motive. Miraculously, all the dessert carnage from across the hall has disappeared. The carpet is spotless.

An old rich couple is already in the elevator when I get on, and they cower in the corner when they see my leather jacket. I'm sure it's the jacket that's causing this reaction. I try to make it better for them by whistling a few bars from 'Streets of Bakersfield,' then lightly singing the lyrics while staring at the mirror in the ceiling; as though I'm alone. As though I'm completely alone: 'Well, you don't know me but you don't like me. You say you care less how I feel. How many of you who sit and judge me have ever walked the streets of Bakersfield.' This isn't working. I can tell it isn't working because the old woman has begun to crouch down behind her husband, protecting her purse. Her fingers are very long and pale, with bulging veins. She clutches her little black satin handbag with rhinestones around the edges. Or maybe they're diamonds. Actual diamonds. *Maybe I should kill them both*, I'm thinking. Murder again.

I cross the lobby through a squadron of fruitcake interior decorator types all dressed in black with ponytails, arranging exotic flowers and puffing up pillows. Very chic people are sinking into paisley overstuffed sofas, reaching for silver trays full of cashews and almonds; some of them flailing about like the furniture's trying to swallow them whole. I come to a dead stop again. Right in the middle of all this. All this luxury. All this murder. I think of Céline. For some reason Céline comes into my mind. The very last question of the very last interview before he died. He was sitting on a park bench in the shade of a hickory tree, wrapped in a raggedy overcoat. He was old and battered. Mutilated by war. He could barely see through the scar tissue piled up around his eyes. The interviewer's last question was: what did he really want in this life? Céline turned to him slowly and said: 'I just want to be left alone.'

3/4/90 (HOLLYWOOD)

Gary Cooper,
or the
Landscape

Why don't you fly? I find that so fascinating.

I don't know. I just don't.

You drive everywhere?

Yes. Or take trains.

I love trains.

Me too.

I used to take them all the time when I was a child, in Sweden. All over Europe.

Yes. They rock you to sleep. Just like a mother.

But say you have to be in Los Angeles suddenly. How do you get there?

I never have to be anywhere suddenly.

But your work – sometimes you must have to work in Los Angeles.

Yes. Then I drive.

Across the entire country?

Right.

How far is that?

It's a long, long way.

It must be thousands of miles.

It is.

So you've done this many times, I guess.

Many, many times.

I've always wanted to do this! I must try it sometime. I've heard so much about this country but never really seen it. You know – I mean other than New York and L.A.

You *should* try it.

Well, what do you do? Is there a particular route you take?

Highway 40 west.

Is that the main highway?

Yes. It replaced the old Route 66. *Grapes of Wrath.* Henry
Fonda. You know – 'Get your kicks on Route 66.'

I see. But aren't there little highways left that might be more
interesting?

What are you interested in?

I mean, the main highway must be so synthetic, isn't it?

They're all made out of asphalt.

No, but I mean the surrounding areas. The little communities.

There *are* no communities.

But there must be some little towns left. Little side roads.

They're all the same.

Aren't there some that are more picturesque? More authentic.

They're *all* authentic.

I see. Well, where do you stay when you're on the road like
that?

I sleep in my truck.

Oh, you have a truck?

I do. Yes.

I love trucks.

Yeah. Trucks and trains.

I just love them.

You should get a truck.

Oh, no!

Why not? Get a truck and drive.

No, no. I'd get so bored with myself, driving all that way alone. Don't you ever get bored?

No.

You travel all by yourself and you never get bored?

Never.

I don't know if I could stand it. All that way across the country. It's so huge! How many days does it take you?

Five usually. Depends. Sometimes I stop along the way.

You must have a lot of girlfriends in different towns.

Not anymore.

Don't you get lonely?

Sometimes.

I would get so lonely, I think.

Yeah. *You* probably shouldn't try it.

Oh, but I must. I feel as though I'm missing out on something. Since I was a little girl I've dreamed about the West.

In Sweden?

Yes! Oh, yes. I used to have visions about it.

Visions.

Vistas would appear.

Where did you hear about the West in Sweden?

Movies. American movies. We see that great landscape in our dreams. It haunts us.

So it's the landscape that grabs you more than the characters?

Yes. That vast background.

So in Sweden, when you're watching an American western, you're all staring at the background? Is that it?

I suppose. It's so evocative to us. All that space. Sweden is very close.

So it doesn't matter who's in the western – it could be John Wayne or Jerry Lewis – because everyone's really captured by the landscape?

Well, we love the actors too, of course.

Who's your favorite?

Mine, personally?

Yes. Do you have a favorite?

I guess I would have to say Gary Cooper.

The Coop!

Oh, yes. He personified something, I think.

What was that?

Excuse me?

That he 'personified.'

Oh, I don't know. That wonderful mixture of shyness – how do you say it? – vulnerability, I suppose, and yet strong at the same time. It's very western. Women love that.

They do?

Oh, yes. It's very attractive, I find.

Why's that?

I don't know. You're making me blush.

I am?

Yes. You know you are.

You're embarrassed?

No. Not exactly.

But when you get right down to brass tacks, which is more important – Gary Cooper or the landscape?

Oh, I would hate to have to choose between them.

Say you had to. Say it was a question of life or death.

I would have to say the landscape.

There you go.

But I love them both.

1/19/94 (NEW YORK CITY)

Spencer Tracy is not Dead

This morning I'm leaving by car for Mexico to shoot a film directed by a German, written by a Swiss, photographed by a Greek, with a crew of Frenchmen and Italians. It should be interesting. A metallic blue Lincoln stretch limo pulls up in front of the hotel, and the chauffeur steps out in full regalia: a tall, blond Viking type in a shiny tuxedo, complete with cummerbund and ruffled chest. His name is Gunther Henker, he's from Austria, and he's a pain in the ass. He drives like he thinks he's still on the autobahn: charging right up on the rear end of the car in front of him and flashing his lights, demanding they get out of his lane. I try to explain to him that when you drive like this in America, all you're going to do is piss people off. He says: 'But zey should move over! Don't zey know zis? Ve are in ze fast lane, not ze slow lane!' He continues with this obnoxious charging tailgate approach. Rednecks in Camaros are flipping us the finger; letting us pass, then running up behind us and blinking their lights in revenge. Some are waving pistols out the window and showing us their hunting knives. I suggest to Gunther that maybe he should take off his tuxedo once we get into Arizona. It might help to take the sting out of this class problem we're running into. He laughs his hearty German laugh: 'In America zere is no class! Isn't zat ze whole idea of America? Everyone ze same! I love it!' He slams the dashboard with his open palm and charges on.

'Yeah, but when you try to cross the Painted Desert in a blue stretch limo, wearing a tuxedo, you're automatically making a statement.'

'No statement. It's simply more professional to wear ze tuxedo. People see ze tuxedo and realize I am a professional. Zey have respect!'

'Well, I'll tell you what – if you still have that cummerbund on by the time we reach West Texas, you might just as well be wearing a chicken suit.' He doesn't laugh. He has no sense of comedy. He is ruthlessly German through and through. He keeps right on hammering through the fast lane, mowing down pickup trucks and low-riders. Luckily, the windows are tinted very dark in the back, so I don't have to suffer the humiliation of being seen with this asshole. I hunker down deep in the back seat, watching the telephone poles go scorching by.

No sooner have we crossed the state line when an Arizona Highway Patrol car comes roaring up behind us with all its Christmas lights popping and the siren full bore. Gunther gives an incredulous look in the rearview mirror, then pulls over, grumbling something in German. 'Just tell him you're a professional.' I can't help rubbing it in. 'He'll be able to tell by your outfit.'

'Any idea how fast you were goin' here, buddy?' the cop says as he leans through the window, trying to get a glimpse of who's in back. (I'm hiding behind a copy of *The Thorough-bred Times*.)

'No, Officer, I really have no idea. I am on a strict schedule. I am working for a company,' says Gunther.

'Well, yer gonna by *behind* schedule if you drive across Arizona at that speed, son, 'cause everybody's gonna haul you over. This thing sticks out like shit on a napkin.'

'Yes, sir. I realize zat,' says Gunther. 'Maybe you'd be willing to close one eye to it?' he says, and gives him the dumbest wink I've ever seen; as though he were attempting to imitate Peter Lorre.

'What's that supposed to mean?' the cop says. 'That supposed to be some kinda bribe or somethin'?'

'No, sir. I was just suggesting –'

'Who owns this car anyhow?' the cop demands.

'Ze company, sir. I am just ze driver. I am a professional driver.'

'Let's see the papers,' says the cop, and Gunther extracts a thick folder crammed with different-colored forms from the glove compartment.

'All's I need's the papers, not the damn instruction book,' says the cop as he snatches the registration out of Gunther's hand. Now we just sit there by the side of the highway while the cop walks back to his squad car and talks on his radio to headquarters.

'No vonder zere is so much crime in America. Everyone here is frustrated by zees laws. In Germany ve drive fast. Zey make an arrangement with ze police. Ze car manufac-turers keep ze autobahn open for high performance engines. Mercedez, BMW, Porsche – zey all make arrangements with ze police. Here you are living in a fascist state.'

'Right. This is exactly the reason I wanted a Chevy.' For some unknown reason the cop lets us off the hook, and we press on toward El Paso. Gunther becomes very silent and sullen, keeping the speedometer pinned at 65. Slowly, he creeps back up into the eighties, and then, before you know it, he's pushing 95 again. Saguaro cactuses are blasting past the windows. The barren land yawns out toward Las Cruces and the cattleyards. We're eating up the miles like a freight train. Gunther isn't talking, which is fine by me. He's sulking still. His neck has become stiff as an oak tree. A Gestapo neck. He doesn't play the radio. He doesn't smoke. His hands stay clamped on the wheel, robot style. His eyes are two steel balls. I peek over the front seat at the speedometer, and sure enough, he's managed to crack 110. Maybe he's decided to kill us both, just out of spite.

As we come roaring into the El Paso border check, there's a roadblock set up. They must have heard we were coming. Somebody must've radioed ahead. There's a whole line of narc cops duded out in green army fatigues, with combat boots, bulletproof vests, and blue baseball caps; all of them armed with machine guns and automatic pistols. German shepherds lunge at the ends of their chains, barking and snarling at the blue limo as we slide to a smoking stop.

'You boys mind steppin' outa the vehicle, please?' the head narc says to us. 'That means you too, pal – you in back,' he says to me. I notice they're all popping the snaps on their holsters that cover the trigger guards. Two narcs are already circling the limo with panting dogs. They must be expecting a world-record bust here or something. 'We're not in Mexico, are we?' I ask one of them, attempting a lame joke. He gives me his best Texas sneer and puts his thumb on the hammer of his nine-millimeter.

'Am I speakin' Spanish, buster?' he says. Gunther is being body searched and having his cummerbund roughly removed. They drop it in the desert dust. They ask me to take my boots off, and I oblige them.

'Them are some fancy boots,' one of them comments.

'Thank you, sir.'

'Cow that went into them boots musta had the measles, huh? What kinda hide you call that?'

'That's belly ostrich, sir.'

'Belly ostrich. I'll be. Ostrich ain't even a cow, is it?'

'No, sir.'

'Ostrich's a damned bird.'

'That's right. I believe it is.'

'Bird boots.'

'Yes, sir.'

'Boots like that must come pretty damn high, huh?'

'Yes, sir.'

'Where'd you come across a pair a bird boots like that?'

'Fort Worth, sir.'

'Fort Worth, Texas?'

'Yes, sir.'

'Must be the best, then. Nothin' but the best for you. Ain't that right?'

'That's absolutely correct, sir.'

'Stretch goddamn limos and bumpy bird boots. Somebody must be livin' right.'

'Somebody must.' The head narc comes strolling up to me, shifting his cartridge belt and rolling his neck slightly. He stares into my forehead as though my eyes were set two inches higher than normal. 'Now, I wanna tell you somethin' here. You see these dogs? These dogs are trained to smell narcotics. That's their job. That's all they're trained for, you understand? Now, when they happen to actually smell narcotics, they go on what we call "alert." See the way he is there – all waggin' and whinin' like that? See how excited he is? That's "alert". Now, it may well be, since this here is a rental-type limo deal – it may very well be that somebody else, who previously rented this car back in la-la-land, might have smoked a marijuana cigarette in the back seat or done himself a line of cocaine. That could well be the case; I'm givin' you the benefit of the doubt, understand? But when one of these dogs goes on "alert," like this here, we are obliged to strip the car down and search it in detail. Have you boys got any objections to that?'

'No, sir,' I say.

'Good. Then pull yer boots back on and just stand over there by the shoulder while we get this thing done.'

Me and Gunther stand there dumbly and watch as they peel the headliner and all the door panels off and lay them out on the steaming blacktop. I'm hopping around on one foot, trying to pull my boots back on, while the dogs leap back and forth over the front seat, rooting their black noses through the fancy upholstery and whining like they're on the trail of a bitch in heat. One of them goes into a fit of barking and starts clawing at the carpeting. The narcs strip all the floor mats and carpet out and lay them on the road. They let all the air out of the tires and pop the hubcaps. They poke through the trunk with their machine guns and give the spare tire a once-over. All our luggage is lined up in the sand, as they rummage through our clothes. It's a little like a gang rape, as I watch my underwear being pillaged. Gunther just keeps adjusting his cummerbund and dusting it off, grumbling to himself and checking his watch. 'We'll never make our schedule now,' he says. 'So zis is your famous America! A police state! Somezing like zis would never happen in Germany. It would never be allowed.'

'Right,' I say. 'You guys really know when to draw the line.'

About an hour and a half later, after they've reassembled our car and filled all the tires back up, we're finally on our way again. I tell Gunther I want to drive the rest of the way to Laredo. I insist. He says it's very unprofessional, but he finally agrees and falls instantly asleep in the back seat, sprawled out like a fallen duke. There's dog hair all over the upholstery, and the limo smells like a kennel. It heaves and lurches on its long wheelbase, and again I wonder about the foresight of a production outfit that could think this hulking monster was more suitable than a plain old Chevy. I slip Ponty Bone and the Squeezetones into the tape deck and roll up the tinted window that separates the chauffeur from the passenger. Things are turned around now. I'm behind the wheel. I feel much better about it. Gunther's sawing logs in the back, dreaming about the autobahn. Cruising to the Squeezetones, I set the cruise control dead on 70. Maybe I was born to be a chauffeur. Maybe that's it. I love this open road.

We pull into the Holiday Inn at Laredo a little past midnight. Gunther's still sacked out, so I leave him there in the parking lot and go into the lobby to check in. The bar's exploding with a live Mexican border band, marimbas and all. Dark-eyed beauties in full rainbow skirts and frilly white blouses are flashing back and forth between the rest room and the bar. Their wide-open sexual excitement and gleaming white teeth as they giggle put all my road fatigue in the background. Mexican couples are dancing right out into the lobby, waving Carta Blanca and yipping like hyenas. None of them has driven a thousand miles with a German maniac to get here. They're having so much fun, it's hard to believe this is actually a Holiday Inn.

The prim lady behind the desk has a message for me from Xavier, the Mexican driver who's supposed to take me the rest of the way down to Veracruz. He says to meet him in the bar; he'll recognize me, he says. He has my description, and apparently I'm the only gringo here. There's local city cops with huge Magnum revolvers strapped to their hips,

standing stone-faced in front of the bar entrance. Their
Chicano eyes are scanning the lobby for trouble. Trouble is
the norm on the border. Trouble is always expected. The
cops study me as I enter; trying to fit my face with some FBI
picture they've got stamped in their minds. They shift their
gun belts around and widen their stances. I slip into the bar,
a criminal guilt beginning to shadow me. The music is
pounding out a polka. The squeezebox player, fighting for
volume, keeps turning up his amplifier. Everybody's rolling
drunk. Couples are glued together in perfect sync, gliding
and weaving through the melee, barely brushing the
whirling scarves and skirts and the sea of bobbing Resistols.
As I approach the bar, Xavier comes up to me and
introduces himself. He's a thickset middle-aged guy with
very tired, sad eyes. Eyes that seem full of regret. He assures
me he's already checked everything out at the border and
we should have no trouble getting through tomorrow
morning. All the papers are in order, he says. He excuses
himself, almost apologizing for being so tired from his drive
from Mexico City. He needs sleep very badly. Tomorrow
we cross into Old Mexico and pick up his partner, who'll
share the driving down to Veracruz. I watch him shuffle
away, winding through the crowded dance floor. A tired
man in the midst of a drunken frenzy. I order a Carta
Blanca and notice Gunther standing in the doorway, across
the room, rubbing his eyes and yawning widely. He's got his
tuxedo jacket slung over his shoulder, and his cummerbund's all rumpled and cocked sideways. He seems to have
no sense of himself being out of place. The Mexicans are
staring at him like he's the gringo from Hell. I raise my
bottle of beer to him across the swirling dancers, but he
doesn't see me. He turns and disappears. That's the last I
ever saw of Gunther.

*

Next morning, we cross the bridge over the Rio into Mexico in Xavier's little Chevy Century. He tells me it's the most expensive car available in Mexico. The back seat's so small my knees are tattooing my chin, but at least it's a Chevy. A Chevy at last! We drive up to the Mexican customs building and go inside. It's like a big warehouse, with old wooden school desks arranged in no particular order. Officials in uniform are moving languidly around in the heat, sorting through immigration forms. Huge propeller fans hang low from the rafters, moving so slowly they have no effect on the temperature whatsoever. Xavier tells me to wait for him by a Formica-topped counter while he talks to two border officials. Again, I'm the only gringo in sight. One of the officials breaks away from Xavier and comes over to me. He asks me in English: 'What's your business in Mexico?'

'I'm an actor. I've come here to act in a movie.' This turns out to be absolutely the wrong thing to have told him. Right away there's trouble. I can tell it in his eyes. The official shakes his head and sniffs at the ground with just the right amount of disdain to put me in my place. He does an about-face and returns to Xavier, spurting in heated-up Spanish that I need a work permit to act in his country. Who did I think I was, just waltzing in here expecting to work in Mexico without a permit? Xavier talks fast, trying to fabricate a story off the cuff that I've only come down here to scout some locations and have a little vacation, but it doesn't fly with the officials. I've already let the cat out of the bag. Xavier persists in my defense, and the officials lead us both into an airless back office, with tall metal filing cabinets surrounding the walls. A very skinny woman in glasses and necktie, with a somber Aztec face, is sitting behind a desk. Me and Xavier stand across from her, as the officials rattle off our situation. Again, the aura of guilt hovers all around me. To be gringo in Mexico is to be automatically guilty. I find myself cursing the era of Porfirio Díaz. Secretly, I want them to know that I am, at heart, a Zapatista. It's too pathetic. As the skinny Aztec lady listens stoically to her lackeys, her hard eyes shift slowly over to mine and she studies my face. There's no hatred in her gaze, just pure objectivity, as though she's reading a page in a book. I'm being scrutinized by a pair of eyes that have peered into many faces in exactly the same way as she's perusing mine right now. My guilt is mounting. There's nothing to be done about it. It's a snowball effect. I'm an actor, not a criminal! Maybe it's the same. Maybe there is some inherent crime attached to pretending. Making a living out of pretending. There's a leather-bound bible on the Aztec lady's desk, mounted on a carved wooden stand. It's opened to the book of Job, and the whole thing is suffocating inside a clear plastic Baggie to keep the dust off. Dust is everywhere. Layers and layers of Mexican dust. Her eyes shift back to the two officials as they come to the end of their little denouncement. She gives me one more steely look, as though making sure I understand the precise feeling of standing on foreign ground – what it's like to be subject to the whims of bureaucracy. She turns to Xavier and explains to him in Spanish that we must go back across to the American side and visit the Mexican consulate. We must obtain a temporary entrance permit from the consulate there before I'm allowed into Mexico. That's all she has to say. We're dismissed with a quick plunge of her eyes back to the work piled up on her desk.

'I thought my papers were supposed to be all in order,' I say to Xavier as we leave the building and head back to the car.

He laughs. 'Yes, but this is Mexico!'

We drive back across the Rio Bravo Bridge to the U.S. side, but the traffic is ten times worse in this direction, because of all the Mexicans going to work for better wages or to shop for American goods. We're stuck on the bridge for a good forty-five minutes, right at the halfway marker that divides our two countries. Our back wheels are in Mexico, the front in the U.S. 'I had no idea I wasn't supposed to tell them I was an actor. Nobody at the production office told me about this.'

'It's just easier if you tell them you're on vacation,' Xavier says.

'I would've been glad to.'

There's a constant flow of people walking from Mexico past our windows as we sit there marooned. Skinny old leathery men on broken-down tricycles with jerry-rigged wagons built onto the fronts. They collect cardboard boxes used for packing televisions in the U.S., then sell them back in Mexico. They gather up aluminum Coke cans, metal wire, used spark plugs; anything America throws away. Whole families toting kids on their backs; no shoes; no possessions of any kind. There's a stoic fatalism in their eyes, born from generations of abject poverty, without the luxury of complaint. I picture Zapata slumped back in the throne chair of Porfirio Díaz, his black Indian eyes burning into the lens of an old box camera, while Villa leers next to him, shoulder-to-shoulder. Their day was short-lived.

We finally locate the Mexican consulate, which looks like an abandoned bank; it has tiled floors, and huge murals of charging horses with flared nostrils surround the space. We're confronted by yet another stern-faced woman official planted behind a metal desk. She listens to Xavier explain our situation, but her face doesn't move an inch. She turns to me and stares.

'So you want to make your money in Mexico?' she says to me.

'No, ma'm. I'm just on a little vacation.' She laughs and

turns back to Xavier, who's got a shit-eating grin on his face. She turns back to me, with no trace of a smile now.

'You people are always coming into Mexico and making millions of dollars, then leaving us with nothing. It's always been like this. Do you think this is fair?' she asks me.

'What people?' I say. Has she got me confused with Guggenheim and Rockefeller?

'You're an actor? Is this true?' she says.

'Well – I have done a little of that in my time.' I'm peeking at Xavier for clues on how to handle this. He blinks and stares at the floor.

'What movies have you been in?' she demands.

'Oh, nothing important. Nothing really big.'

'What are the titles? Name some of your movies.'

'You've probably never heard of them,' I say.

'We may be more sophisticated in Laredo than you might expect,' she says, her face growing hard as stone.

'Well – I was in a couple of westerns: *Last of the Comancheros, Fandango Moon;* things like that.'

'*Fandango Moon!*' She lights up. 'You were in *Fandango Moon!*' Her entire personality changes. Suddenly, she transforms into a giggling teenager. 'I can't believe it! That's one of my favorites! I have the video!'

'Well, I'll be darned.'

'No, it's not true. What part did you play? I watch it all the time. What was your character?'

'Um – I played the part of the veterinarian. It was a low-budget type of deal.'

'You were the veterinarian? You were? No, I can't believe this! Yes! You *were* the veterinarian! I recognize you now!' She starts yelling with abandon across the cavernous room to another woman sitting behind a metal desk: 'Maria! Mira, Maria! He was in *Fandango Moon*! He played the veterinarian! Look! It's him!' She grabs hold of my hand and looks deep into my eyes like a little girl. 'What's your name?' she says in a kind of low purr. Xavier has backed away from her desk in confusion. His hands, clasped in front of his belt, hold the forms that he's carried from the border control. He seems completely bewildered by this shift of attitude and out of his depth. 'What's your name?' she persists.

'My name is Spencer Tracy,' I tell her.

'Spencer Tracy? It's Spencer Tracy, Maria!' she screams across the room, then catches herself and looks hard at my face, as though studying one of her immigration forms. 'Spencer Tracy the actor? No.'

'Yes, ma'm. The very one.'

'No, but you're famous, I know that. I've seen you. What's your real name? Spencer Tracy is dead.'

'Nope. He's very much alive.'

At this point, all the secretaries and women officials, led by Maria, are prowling toward me like people who've heard there's a car wreck. 'Maria! Spencer Tracy is dead, isn't he? Isn't he dead?' Maria is totally stumped, but she's clutching a little scrap of notepaper and a pen, just in case I'm somebody. The woman behind the desk clutches my arm now, pulling me toward her. 'Can I have your autograph? I must have your autograph. I'm going to frame it.' She's doing weird things with her eyes, trying to present herself to me as a potential piece of ass. This is the same woman who, moments before, was ready to crucify me as an American devil. The movies hold a strange international hypnosis, as though real life were suddenly suspended into fantasy land.

'I'll make you a deal,' I say. 'I'll swap you straight across. You get the autograph, and I get my little pink temporary entry permit. How's that? Does that sound fair?'

'Bueno,' she says, and shoves a notepad toward me, with a pen on a chain.

'No. First I get the permit; then you get the autograph.'

She smiles slyly at me. 'So, you don't trust me? All right,' she says. 'It's a deal.' She begins rustling papers and sliding her typewriter around. '*Fandango Moon*! He was the veterinarian!' she repeats to all the secretaries. 'Don't you recognize him?' They all shake their heads, but some of them shyly hold out their little slips of paper and ballpoint pens.

'Why do you want my autograph when you don't even recognize me?' I ask them.

'Because you're famous. You're Spencer Tracy.'

Xavier has removed himself completely by now and pretends to be sorting through the forms he's holding, taking peeks now and then to see if this deal is actually going through. Finally, I get the little pink permit, and I give her the autograph. She stares at it in bewilderment. 'Can you print your name beside it? I can't read this,' she says.

'What do you mean, print my name? It's supposed to be a signature. That's what an autograph is. It's a signature.'

'I know, but I can't read it. What good is it if I can't read it? Nobody will even know who it is.'

'It's possible they won't know anyway,' I tell her, waving the little pink permit as me and Xavier say adiós.

We drive back across the border and reenter the customs building. Our friend the grim official is smacking his lips and making a big sweaty smile at us as he sees the permit dangling from my hand. He rubs his palms together and hitches up his belt like he's about to sit down to dinner. Then he stamps the little pink paper and gives me thirty days entry. He has no idea what I went through to get this thing.

We drive into Nuevo Laredo and pick up Phillipe, the backup driver, at a very seedy cinder-block motel. Phillipe has a dark Indian face with sad, gentle eyes. We weave our way out of town through the narrow, broken streets. The Mexican atmosphere devours the last remnants of American commercialism: A Shell gas station with green and red lightning designs girdling the fuel pumps; a Coke sign fringed with rattling tinfoil strips. Ancient Indian men in broad sombreros and white pajamas sit, leaning on their sotol canes next to children who play reed flutes. Women in slinky red satin dresses and black high heels lean into peeling archways, looking like they've got no place to go and could care less. Old women, hunched over, their heads covered in blue fringed shawls, shuffling barefoot up the dusty streets. Broken-down buses with gold chains and crucifixes swinging wildly from the sun visors. Vendors hawking cactus candy and blue ice drinks. Bony dogs lapping at the gutter water. Pachucos with their sleeves rolled up, sporting handmade tattoos of the Virgin and the name of some girl. Chickens in wooden cages. Scarves with the map of Mexico embroidered in red, hanging from hemp ropes. Pigs' heads bleeding from steel hooks. Movie house marquees with titles all about death. Death and Love. Love and Death. Suddenly, everything is human, and America has gone away.

Xavier drives like a man possessed. He makes Gunther seem like a little old lady from Pasadena. There are no real rules for the Mexican highways. Even traffic lights are wide open to improvisation. The roads are like continuous disaster zones: huge cannonball craters appear without warning; no brightly painted orange lines dividing lanes; no reflectors marking shoulders that can sometimes drop straight off into Hell itself. Burros, horses, cattle, sheep, goats, wander back and forth, sometimes grazing smack in the middle of the road. People on foot and bicycles wobble under huge loads of fire-wood and pottery. Often, the busted blacktop abruptly quits and turns into gravel or mud. In the mountains, the road squeezes down into a single-lane switchback with sheer drops of dizzying height, plunging into the tropical rain forest below. Xavier's technique is to pass on every sharp curve with the pedal to the metal, blinking the lights furiously and blaring the horn. He's absolutely fearless in this. He'll pass three or four cars in one lick, heading straight into a blind curve. If a car appears suddenly in the opposing lane, he just bullies his way over, cutting in front of the car he's just passed. Nobody seems offended by this method. Xavier says it's simple intimidation. They see it's a new car and the most expensive kind in Mexico. 'They believe I'm a diplomat or part of the government!' He laughs. At least he's not wearing a tuxedo.

On the outskirts of Monterrey, we pull off into a gravel apron where six policemen are pushing a broken-down Volkswagen. Why it takes six of them, I don't know. Maybe it's their sense of community. Phillipe takes over the wheel and asks the cops how to get on the alternate route that skirts Monterrey, so we don't have to crawl through the congested center of town. All the cops are puffing and sweating, and each one seems to have a different idea about the best road to take. Phillipe listens patiently, then decides to take his own course, which he figures out on the map. As we swing back onto the highway, we get stuck behind a rickety mule-drawn wagon with the words *I Mexican* painted in red and orange across the back. All along the road approaching Monterrey, vendors are offering baby goats, holding them high above their heads and twisting them from side to side so that their long ears flap against the sky. More vendors line the road, selling long ropes of garlic, raw pottery stacked on their heads, hand-tooled wallets and belts, inner tubes, batteries, candy. It's an open market. Xavier spots an Indian family, the mother and kids trotting along, trying to keep up with the father. He begins to tell me about his children and how he misses them. He hasn't seen them for a month, having to take on extra work due to a crisis he recently survived. He was sitting in his little office in the heart of Mexico City one afternoon, when two hooded gunmen burst in and slammed him to the floor. They put machine guns to his head and told him to take all his clothes off. They tied him up naked and gagged, then cleaned him out of every piece of office equipment he owned: computers, typewriters, phones, even the desk and chairs. He says it had taken him ten years to amass all this stuff. Then they placed the barrels of their guns in each of his ears and told him if he informed the police or attempted to chase them they'd blow his brains out. They left with all his booty stuffed into his second-best car (this Chevy Century was out on a job) and disappeared. Xavier remained bound and gagged through the night on the floor, buck naked in a bare office. He wasn't found until the next morning, by Phillipe.

'Mexico City is full of thieves,' he says. 'They will kill you for a pair of shoes.'

The road gets worse up into the mountains outside Tampico, as night comes down. Patches of dense fog clear suddenly, to reveal old men on burros towing cattle along behind them with frayed ropes. The old men are sound asleep in the saddle, their huge sombreros nodding along in rhythm to the burros' trot. Xavier is back behind the wheel and presses on relentlessly, pushing the little Chevy to its limits. He passes three gravel trucks on a blind curve at eighty miles an hour. This has been a grueling seven hundred miles from Nuevo Laredo to Poza Rica, just outside Veracruz. The suspension keeps slamming up into the floorboards as we lurch down the side of the mountain. Xavier doesn't blink. He is a man of iron. Phillipe sleeps beside him, hands folded in his lap. We are, all three, silent now, crashing through the night deep into the luxuriant jungle. Voices of parrots and long-tailed grackles break out to us from far below. It's a long way from L.A.

We approach the oil refineries of Poza Rica about 1:00 a.m. Tall plumes of orange flame brighten the night into an eerie glow, and the smell of oil blankets everything. We're all half starved, and there's only one little cantina open in town, so we hit it. The only thing they have to eat at this hour is something called bolinas, a kind of deep-fried fritter with chicken and egg in the middle. It's fried in pork grease and tastes like rancid popcorn but great on an empty stomach. This café is open to the street and faces out on a beautiful zócalo, where the grackles are squawking loudly and flapping around through a carob tree. There's a color TV above the bar, blasting out an inane comedy where two transvestites are trying to rob a bank. Phillipe and Xavier are mixing up a drink with Nescafé and boiled milk, adding tons of white sugar. The town is empty except for us.

In my hotel room I find a note from the director, saying the whole company has decided to move to a small hotel in Papantla, the next town over, and deeper in the jungle. I'm welcome to join them there tomorrow. There's a huge basket of tropical fruit and a bottle of champagne beside the note. I drain the whole bottle and crash. I have 'temporarily' arrived.

3/8/90 (HOLLYWOOD TO POZA RICA, MEXICO)

Opuestos

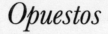

Why are you always crossing the river? What do you do over there, anyway?

I like it.

Yes, but what do you do? Why were you gone all day today, for instance?

Los gallos.

What?

Los gallos.

Don't talk Mexican to me! You know I can't stand that.

Roosters.

That's why you come back splattered in chicken blood and smelling like a dead man? Chicken fights?

Sí. Los gallos.

What is that awful smell you always come back with?

Sotol.

That white stuff?

Sotol coyame. Homegrown.

Why does it make you smell like that?

Cactus.

I don't understand you.

No. It's true.

I never will understand you.

Probably not.

Who are these women in the back of the truck?

Gabriel's sisters.

Sure.

They are. Ask them.

I don't speak Spanish.

Ask them in English. They'll tell you.

You were gone all day with them?

They rode in back.

Now you come back and it's already night. Pitch-black night.

They rode in back. They sat on the spare tires the whole way. Just like they're sitting now; wrapped in blankets. Ask Gabriel.

What did you do over there with them?

I told you.

Cockfights? That's all you did? Watch a bunch of poor dumb chickens rip each other to ribbons?

We stopped and bought a mule.

A mule?

A white one. He just appeared behind a salt cedar and we saw him. Pure white.

Why are you always going over there? Can't you find what you want in Texas?

Texas is tame.

Tame?

Yes.

'Texas is tame'? That's your answer?

I have no answer.

I'm going back.

Jump in the truck.

I'm *walking* back.

Come on, jump in the truck. You can ride up in front.

Oh, so *I* can ride in front! What about your Mexican girls?

They ride in back. To them, we're still in Mexico. Siempre en Mexico. They don't care about the river.

I'm walking.

Wait a minute. I'll walk with you.

I'm walking alone.

Was that you singing before? Out here on the sandbar?

Don't follow me. I'm walking alone! You stay here with your Mexican girls.

Beautiful singing. We stopped the truck to cool the oil down before we crossed back over, and we heard this singing. At first I thought it was livestock. Then it sounded human.

It *was* human. It was me.

What were the words?

I was singing in order to feel less alone. It's spooky out here at night. There's bats flying just above the water.

But now I'm back.

Yeah. And I feel more alone than ever.

You're walking away from me, that's why.

Why can't you just stay home!

You should come over with me sometime. You'd like it.

Mexico scares me. I've told you that.

But why?

I don't speak the language.

That's no reason.

Everything about it terrifies me. I always think I'm about to be murdered over there.

Even in the open?

Yes. Even more so in the open. The plants. The animals. Even the rocks are terrifying.

You're not afraid of rocks?

No. It's what they imply. This menacing wildness. All humans are foreigners over there. Even Mexicans. You have no business going over there all the time. One day you'll be killed. Wait and see.

I mind my own business. I never insult anyone.

You're riding with Mexican women. That's already an insult to them.

They're Gabriel's sisters!

That's what *you* say.

Just jump in the truck.

Why don't you just go live over there if you like it so much! Why even bother coming back?

I come back because of you.

Why me? I'm the opposite of you.

Maybe that's it.

1/29/95 (SAN CARLOS, MEXICO)

Lost in the Ruins

First day of shooting, and I realize I have no idea whatsoever how to play this character. Usually, by this time, there's some slight inkling at least; some impulse. I've been waiting for something to start taking place inside me, but nothing's visited so far. I've read the novel that the screenplay's based on. I've taken notes. I've read the screenplay several times. Taken more notes. But still, nothing. Somewhere, I read that Laurence Olivier said he liked to start with something from the outside and work his way in. Something very simple and obvious, like a limp or a facial twitch or a speech mannerism, and then allow that to work its way into the emotional life of the character. Maybe I should try a limp, although there's nothing in the material that even vaguely suggests lameness. I don't know what to do. I get dressed up in the costume. This is the first time I've put all the clothes on as an ensemble. Maybe something will happen. The fancy handmade English shoes; the tiny Italian tailor's perfect slacks; the period watch; the snakeskin belt. Still, nothing comes. Through the curtains in my trailer I can see a group of little Mexican boys with their reed flutes, jumping up and down outside my window and yelling at me to buy them and take them back with me to America. I put on the period hat and the period glasses. Something very distant starts to happen. This is a man who wears glasses and a hat! A minor revelation, but it's better than nothing. This is a man who wears a watch! He cares about time. He wears handmade English shoes. He's got some scratch! I stare at the shoes. They remind me of Robert Morley in John Huston's *Beat the Devil*. What period was that movie? Earlier. Had to be thirties; late thirties. This one is supposed to be the fifties. I remember the fifties. I lived through the fifties, but it doesn't help. My memories of the fifties have nothing to do with this character's. I remember great Chevys with fins and Tijuana girls in tight split skirts. That's about it. Something about *Beat the Devil* strikes a chord. European sleazy characters stranded in an exotic environment. Similar to this. Dust. Bogart. Peter Lorre. Brecht. No! Not Brecht! Don't get off the track here. It must be the German influence that's causing this. Maybe I'll try out a walk. Just for the heck of it. Just a simple walk. Nothing fancy. I start pacing the aisle of the trailer in full costume, with the suit coat slung over my shoulder. I'm hoping a walk will emerge. A particular walk, characteristic of the character. A walk that feels unlike my own walk yet close enough that I won't feel stupid doing it. I feel stupid enough already in this getup, with no clue who I'm supposed to be. Out of the corner of my eye I catch the orphan kids' heads popping up and down at the window, laughing at my walk. There's a knock on my trailer door. The first of many to come. They want to see me in the makeup trailer. I haven't even found my walk yet, and they want me for makeup!

From my trailer to the makeup trailer I walk my normal walk through dozens of Tohacatec Indian extras and the group of little boys who now grab at my sleeves and ask me to buy them. Now, suddenly, I begin to feel something coming! This character is European through and through. Western. American, and gringo to the bones. He's in a foreign land, but he carries all his baggage with him; all his curse of heritage. His sense of superiority is involuntary. Intellectual. It's culturally preordained. He looks into the faces of these Indians without the slightest empathy. They are victims of culture, the same as him. Victims of the jungle; he, of the industrial age. They have nothing in common. He feels no contempt; just indifference. He's not as soft as Robert Morley, yet not as hard as Bogart. He's simply alone.

The first shot is a relatively simple one from the actor's standpoint but a nightmare for the director. It's a drive-up where me and a German character actor named Hendker are supposed to arrive on the site of an archaeological dig in this beat-up International Harvester truck with a burned-out clutch. The camera begins on the site of the ruins, with dozens of Indian laborers crawling all over the pyramids, carrying stones from one place to another. Then me and Hendker drive into the scene, and the shot ends. Not much acting involved. Simple. Just drive the truck. The Tohacatec extras are direct descendants of the original tribes who built these pyramids. In real life they work for the Mexican government, doing exactly the same kind of labor that they're now being asked to do for the camera. Only problem is they have no conception of the repetition of film work. Once they've completed a task, it's inconceivable to them that they have to do the whole thing over again in exactly the same way. They stand there and stare at the camera while the assistant directors explain to them in Spanish over bullhorns that they shouldn't look at the camera when they're being photographed. 'Under no circumstances look at the camera! Comprende?' Another problem arises: the Tohacatec don't speak Spanish. The ADs consult with bilingual Indian officials, who explain the whole thing over again to the extras, this time in their own language. They still don't get it. Why not look at the camera? It's there. It's staring them right in the face. They can see their own image reflected back at them through its myopic glass eye. It's a very curious object, but they should pretend it doesn't exist? They become extremely confused. Their eyes dart around now, trying to avoid the black Arriflex like children who've been warned not to stare at a naked woman. They become ashamed. They stare at the ground. They stare at their callused feet. They've rehearsed the shot ten times now, and they're beat.

Me and Hendker are parked in the International deep in the jungle, with a walkie-talkie on the seat between us, awaiting our cue to enter the scene. We've been waiting here for half an hour now, while they've been trying to resolve this Indian labor conundrum. The humidity is so high that the headliner of the truck is sweating. Our socks are dripping wet. Makeup is running down our collars and staining our white shirts a pale piss orange. The makeup team is frantic, changing our shirts and mopping up all the sweat with little yellow sponges. Finally, the cue arrives – the crackling, hysterical voice of the assistant director through the walkie-talkie: '*Action!*' Hendker floors the truck, and we come charging out of the jungle underbrush, but the clutch is really smoking bad and the International begins to buck wildly as we come lurching onto the scene in fits and spurts. It would make a great entrance for Laurel and Hardy, but this is a serious German film. The Indians drop their heavy stones and stare at us as the pathetic old truck convulses to a halt, surrounded by gray smoke. The director has now lost it completely. He's yelling at the whole set: 'Am I dreaming!' he screams. 'Is this a nightmare I'm having! Why is the truck smoking! I didn't ask for that! Why are they all still staring at the camera! I've told them not to look at the camera! Everyone's told them! We've rehearsed this a dozen times, and they're still staring into my lens! I can't believe it!' The second AD is running like a mad a dog toward the Indian interpreters, pleading with them for co-operation from the extras. Two burly teamsters from Los Angeles are pushing the crippled International back to its starting mark. One of them says to the other, 'This is the first shot of the first day, right?'

'Yeah, right,' the other one gasps.

'Gonna be a long shoot.'

3/12/90 (TAJIN RUINS, MEXICO)

Lajitas and the NFL

This time of year, the Mexicans know a low spot on the Rio Grande where they can cross their skinny ponies and ride up to the trading post in Lajitas, on the U.S. side of the border. Nobody bothers them. Nobody asks to see papers or questions their motives. They're regular visitors. This same low spot is the reason General John J. Pershing established his little fort here in 1916, in his vain attempt to bring Pancho Villa to his knees. He never got close enough to even see the dust of Villa's army. The infamous Comanche Trail also encountered this shoal in the river, where for more than a hundred years the Comanche raided like clockwork under the full moon and vanished with their booty into the vast plains of Chihuahua. Today these Mexican villagers have simply come to hear some cantina music on an old Wurlitzer jukebox, drink Bud Light, then return to San Carlos, seventeen miles into Old Mexico. As they arrive at the trading post, their eyes squint toward the

213

patio, draped for some reason in black plastic sheets. Gringos in funny hats are crowded around a TV set in the center of a dusty old pool table. These gringos cheer in unison, then fall deathly silent, then cheer again. Their eyes are nailed to the tiny screen, watching the NFC playoff game between Dallas and San Francisco. They are totally oblivious to the ragged little band of men on mud-splattered ponies trotting up behind them. The Mexicans drop the reins of their bony horses into mesquite bushes and dismount. They don't even tie them. The horses know the routine. The men go directly into the grocery store and buy a case of beer, then shyly come back out into the plastic shade of the patio. They quietly seat themselves on a wood bench like a row of crows on a wire, their straight backs flat against the cool adobe wall of the store. Their eyes are careful not to meet the gaze of the gringos in funny hats. They care nothing about American football. They're only here for la musica and Bud Light.

The black visqueen sheets ripple gently in the desert wind. Goats bleat from a pen devised from hubcaps and barbed wire at the back of the store. You can see their spotted legs through the gaps of the billowing plastic. The Mexicans pop their beers, and their dark eyes shift toward the TV image of Troy Aikman in close-up. His very white Viking face barking out the play pattern. He drops into a boot-leg left to Emmitt Smith, who darts through the 49er defense and is about to break into open field, when his chronic hamstring seizes him and he drops like he's been shot. The gringos in funny hats bolt to their feet in unison, an enraged, many-headed beast, cursing and moaning in chorus as though Emmitt's sudden relapse was somehow deeply personal and beyond football; beyond a mere game. This moaning echoes out over the Rio Grande like the loss of manhood itself. The Mexicans are silent; absolutely still. Very slowly they sip their beer and smile at the gray caliche floor, almost embarrassed to be in the presence of such bewildering madness. The gringos are now angrily crushing their beer cans and throwing money on the picnic tables; punching garbage cans; stomping their funny hats in the dirt. The Mexicans say nothing. Not even in Spanish. They just stare at the floor. Their horses shift weight and twitch their ears toward the roar of the rankled Texans. A crow hops down and struts through the dusty parking lot, then stops and pecks at a half-eaten hot dog.

The replay of Smith's injury in slow motion shows his massive piston legs stretched to their limit, then a freeze-frame reveals the exact moment of pain. His face contorts into a mask of agony, then the film continues into his sudden crash to earth. Again, the Dallas gringos moan and groan, reliving their bad luck, cursing their mothers and sons. The Mexicans grow even more stoic and almost invisible, dissolving into the cool adobe wall until just their black Indian eyes float above the wooden bench. The TV goes into a spasm of static and horrible hissing, desperately trying to link up the immense distance between rainy San Francisco and this remote edge of the world. Territories that have nothing in common. Territories joined, only for a moment, by this game about territory. A national obsession. More than a river divides the dark men the bench from the gringos in funny hats.

The sun begins to drop behind the jagged buttes of Chihuahua. The temperature takes a dip. Geese fly down-river, silhouetted black against the pink fading sky. The fourth quarter looks bleak for Dallas. Aikman's eyes now have the dull recognition of imminent defeat. His helmet is dripping with Candlestick mud, and swaths of slimy green turf are branded across his backside. It's too little too late for the Cowboys. Already, the humbled group of Dallas fans have begun to abandon their funny hats and shuffle off toward pickup trucks, casting last-minute aspersions back toward the TV set. The Mexicans watch them leave. They don't get up from their bench until the last Texan has ground his angry tires in the gravel and disappeared over the sharp rise. They listen to the fading engines, waiting for the air to clear, then, suddenly, the whole line of men is on its feet and dancing. Spanish fills the space. They snap off the TV set, and the hyper, pumped-up enthusiasm of John Madden's voice is replaced by the ancient jukebox. Now all the Mexicans are laughing as the sun sinks deeper, forging broad crimson bands behind the black buttes of their homeland. A dog barks from the Mexican side of the Great River. A confused rooster crows. A pig squeals, and the laughter and music is gobbled up into a silence so complete a man can suddenly hear his own heart.

1/15/95 (LAJITAS, TEXAS)

Papantla

Phillipe drives me over to the little Hotel Tajín in Papantla, where the director is staying. Apparently, he's come down with 'la turista' so bad that he can't get out of bed, but he still wants to see me. Our car climbs the road through the lush jungle with orange groves carved into the steep hillsides. Banana trees are dripping in the humidity; mangos, corn, papayas, jacaranda and bougainvillea lace through the mountainside, completely wild. Green parrots scream from the deep verandas of every hacienda. Even broken-down little stick shacks seem to have a pet parrot squawking from a cage.

Dirt-poor Indians, dressed in white pajamas and mossy green sombreros, are milling around the lobby of the hotel, selling beads. One of the men has grossly deformed feet, with toes that are all grown together, forming a kind of paw. Gigantic feet, like elephantiasis. I don't see how he can get his pants on over these feet, or maybe he never takes them off.

The director descends the staircase, looking very weak and green. He has a good attitude about it; says he thinks he needs to eat something very hot, like chiles pequeños. He knows a fish restaurant not too far from the hotel. We go there and find a table looking out on the open street to a movie marquee that reads: *Buscamos a Ver la Muerte,* with a hand-painted poster of two dark lovers in a passionate embrace, each holding a dagger poised behind the other one's back. The director peruses the menu with slow, deliberate movements, reminding me of the time I was stricken with this very same horrible dysentery in Campeche, back in 1965. I remember lying on a bare mattress, staring up at a slow black ceiling fan and wishing I were dead. It was the only time I've ever actually wished I were dead, and I wished it with all my heart. I ask him if he's getting any medication for it, and he nods vaguely, then wipes a band of sweat off his upper lip. He recommends a particular kind of redfish on the menu, but all I order is a bottle of Carta Blanca and lime. He orders the fish for himself and stares at it for a long time on the plate, moving the massive head around with his fork until it breaks off at the spine. The head has a piranha-like jaw with spiky teeth.

Between bites, he begins to volunteer his feelings to me about the subject of our film: how the novel we're adapting has certain themes that relate directly to his personal life – mainly his problems with women. As he chews his fish, his eyes take on a confessional glaze, as though I'm the first person on earth he's ever revealed these things to. He tells me of a great love he once had and how it got all fucked up through his own failure to see the legitimacy of the woman's point of view. Slowly, in the course of his story, his whole attitude shifts completely, until he ends up blaming her for everything – even his present sickly condition. He concludes by saying that the main problem was that she kept insisting he didn't love her as much as she loved him. 'How could she say that?' he explodes. 'How could she know how much I loved her? How could she possibly measure something like that!' His eyes well up with real hurt, like the way a boy can be injured for life, and he begins to cry into his redfish. The tears drip into the charred eyehole of the severed head. I barely know this man.

In my new room I find a large bottle of clear white Tequila Sauza sitting on the side table. A gift from the company. There's a little balcony that looks directly down on the narrow cobbled streets of Papantla. Two federales in dark green fatigues, machine guns slung over their shoulders, patrol the streets. They smoke and chuckle to each other. They saunter with the arrogance of all men who carry weapons where no one else is allowed to. Papantla is considered part of the Cocaine Corridor, and there's sporadic, unexplained gunfire echoing from the jungle night and day.

My room is blue and green and very small, with a bathroom built like a narrow tile closet, the toilet and shower all in one. The shower emits only a little trickling piss of cold water, and there's a small cell-like window in it, open to the street. No glass. No curtain. As you stand under this cold trickle, you watch it run down your knees onto the white tile and then drain away toward the toilet, where it forms a little gray bubbling pool before it sucks down the grate. At the same time, you're listening to the street below, just outside the little window. It's as close as you could come to actually taking a shower in the middle of the road. You hear children as though you were down there with them. Dogs. You hear tropical bird voices. Spanish. Teenagers in love. Girls giggling. Singing. Distant machine guns. Radios.

You hear Elvis Presley as the tiny bar of soap crumbles into a million bits in your white hand.

At daybreak the grackles wake me up. I find black coffee in a corner café, where a family of peasant men is standing around a table, sombreros in hand. They are placing hot milk and pan dulce in front of a little girl dressed in a navy blue school uniform. She is seated at the table, while all the men remain standing. There are no women with them, just this little girl. The men are dressed in ragged work shirts, white trousers with rope belts, and huaraches with tire treads for soles. They have the dark Indian eyes that look only inward; self-contained. Their hands have seen nothing but hard work. The little girl is spotless. Her glistening patent-leather shoes are perched on a rung of the chair. Her long black hair is washed and combed to perfection; not a strand of it is out of place. Her schoolbooks hang by a belt from the back of her chair. The men gently stroke the top of her head as she bites into the crisp sweet bread and sips her hot milk. Their huge leathery hands barely skim her perfect mane. She is their little saint. She doesn't smile. Her face remains solemn, almost beatific, even as flakes of the sweet bread tumble from the corners of her tiny mouth. The men speak very softly to her, almost whispering, sweetly, as though offering short prayers. They stroke her shoulders and back, barely touching the fabric of her pressed uniform. They move the cup of milk and the basket of bread a little closer to her so she doesn't have to reach. They dab her little chin with a paper napkin and flick away crumbs from her lap. Suddenly, she sees the school bus approaching the zócalo. She leaps to her feet and grabs her books. The men lay coins on the table and escort her outside. Through the window I can see them kissing the top of her soft head and then waving good-bye as they put her on the bus. They stand there as a group, waving in unison until the bus pulls away.

They keep waving until the bus has completely disappeared, then they all shake hands as men and go off in different directions, heading for hard work.

In the zócalo, I sit on a green iron bench under the shade of a huge catalpa tree. Black squirrels carry rotten oranges in their mouths, back and forth from tree to tree. I can't see where they're hiding them. A group of barefooted Indian men in straw hats, long machetes swinging from their belts, cross the plaza and head toward the Catholic church on the corner. The church is set up on a little hill, with a stone wall on two sides of it. The wall has a giant mosaic winged dragon carved into it. A serpent dragon with gaping teeth, bulging eyes, and a long tongue licking out of it. The men in the straw hats pause in front of the dragon and stare up at its mouth. They remove their hats and smile at the teeth. One of them points with his tattered hat to the eye of the serpent. They speak softly to one another in a language I've never heard. The church bell strikes three short gongs that sound like they're being amplified through a broken toy speaker. The men put their hats back on and walk off toward the thick jungle, machetes swinging. Turkeys are gobbling in the distance. One of them shrieks as if it's being chased. A telephone rings in the midst of this, but not with that electronic beep that you hear in the high-tech offices of L.A. This is a ring like phones used to make back in the thirties and forties. A ring that might have come out of a Raymond Chandler movie. It keeps right on ringing, as old women in bright pink, gold-trimmed skirts cross in front of me, carrying plastic containers wrapped in banana leaves on their heads. They dodge a beat-up blue taxi and cross the street, giggling to one another. Bony dogs prowl the zócalo, sniffing for scraps. A slat-sided truck pulls up by the marketplace, and three men jump out and start unloading a decapitated white pig. The letters *CV* are stamped in blue on the hip of the carcass. Another man, in the bed of the truck, tosses the head of the pig into a plastic bucket and lowers it to the street on a rope. The head sloshes around in its own blood.

Later, from the balcony of the Café Centro, the sun is slowly setting over the zócalo and the church with the serpent wall. Evening is closing in. Our film company has taken over a long table overlooking the street and the whole plaza. The view is better than any movie. Tequila and Carta Blanca are flowing freely, and there's almost a holiday feeling among the cast and crew.

On the plaza in front of the church is a wooden pole that rises over a hundred feet into the darkening sky. A small group of Totaneco Indians are gathered at the base of the pole, preparing for a daily ritual. There are five chosen ones among them, called the voladores (flying men), dressed in deep red costumes and headdresses. They begin shimmying up the pole, trailing thick yellow ropes tied around their torsos. An assistant on the ground helps uncoil the ropes, making sure there's no kinks in them. None of the citizens of Papantla seem the least bit interested in this procedure. They never look up. There are very few tourists here, Papantla being so remotely cut off by the jungle. This is simply a daily practice of the Totaneco that's been going on so long nobody can remember when it started. The voladores keep climbing higher, to the very top of the pole, with no fanfare. The last one up is a boy of about ten years old. When they arrive, the leader sits on the very tip of the pole and begins playing a bamboo flute with one hand and a small drum with the other. His balance is impeccable. The other four position themselves on a wooden ring that surrounds the pole; they begin removing the ropes from around their chests and tying them to their ankles. As the leader continues his haunting flute music, the whole thing begins to take on the aura of an exotic circus act, except there are no guide wires, no harnesses, no safety nets, and no real audience except us: a bunch of gringo fools trying to make a movie. The moment the sun sets fully, down behind the palm trees, the leader suddenly stands on the tip of the pole and begins to dance in tight circles, while continuing to play the flute and the drum. It's an amazing thing. The tip of the pole can't be any more than four inches in diameter and he's somehow dancing on it. He crouches over in the style of the North American thunderbird, pounding his feet down and whipping his body to the left and right. Then, on some silent signal or a cue from the music, the other four throw themselves backward into the night sky and 'fly.' The ropes slowly uncoil around the axis of the small wooden frame they've been sitting on, and they sail in ever-widening circles, hanging by their ankles. The young boy seems the freest and most daring. He spreads his arms wide and rolls over, with his mouth wide open. His whole face is smiling. His eyes are closed in ecstasy, and the rising moon seems to slip through his head as he circles slowly to earth.

A dark, Apache-looking man sits down across from me at the table and introduces himself: Raul Cantado. He's a veteran stuntman, but the director's given him a small role in this film as some kind of favor. Raul began his career as a bullfighter in Tijuana, then moved into stunt doubling and, at once point, became the stand-in for the legendary Mexican actor-director Emilio Fernandez – who played Mapache in Peckinpah's *The Wild Bunch*. Fernandez gained notoriety for having shot three people in his life, the last one being a critic who'd had the temerity to give him a bad review. Apparently, Emilio had just been released from prison for his second murder; went directly to the critic's house; rang the doorbell; and shot him in the head when he answered. According to Raul, Fernandez always showed up on the set of a movie with a snake-skin briefcase containing his script, a bottle of white tequila, and his .45 pistola. His career came to an abrupt end when he brought three hookers home one evening and ordered his wife to cook for them. She shot him in the throat with his own gun.

Raul likes to drink a lot of tequila and tell stories. He drinks more tequila than ten men. He says he was born in Eagle Pass, Texas, on the Rio Grande border. His father was a Catholic priest and his mother was a Chiricahua Apache. A similar background to my favorite poet, César Vallejo. Raul's never heard of him. He says, 'Poets are women.' For years he did horse stunts on John Ford westerns up in Monument Valley, and he shows me the ragged scars on his knees and shins from all the saddle drags. He wears a long black ponytail that falls down between his shoulder blades, but the top of his head is completely bald. More scars run down his arms and across his thick wrists. His silver-and-turquoise rings clink against his glass of tequila as he raises it and toasts: 'Hasta noverte mío Dios!' We all drink as the moon rises full and the trashed-out taxis squeal around the zócalo below us.

Down on the dark street, I do my best to escort Raul back to the hotel. His eyes are in the back of his head and he's walking like a first-calf heifer, about to have it. He's a short man, well into his fifties but powerful in every respect. He has a neck like Mike Tyson and legs of iron. He keeps crashing into lampposts and trees, then coming to a dead stop, eyes swimming, trying to focus on the object he's just had a wreck with. As we careen past the church wall, Raul stops to stare at the mouth of the giant serpent. He gazes up at the teeth and the snakelike tongue. He says he would like a woman right now. He would like her to just appear before him, standing there naked with her breasts dripping. It's 3:00 a.m., and the zócalo's completely empty. Not even a cat or a whimpering dog. He says he wants to go to the whorehouse now. He knows one right around the corner, he says. 'All of them young. Jove y duro,' he says. I keep tugging on his elbow, trying to steer him toward the hotel, and he calls me a coward. 'Women will turn you into a coward! A coward of life! They will make you less than a man!'

We crash into the lobby of the hotel, and the sleeping desk clerk jumps to his feet, knocking over the telephone, which makes a dull ring when it hits the tile floor, then shatters. The clerk curses as he gets down on his knees, trying to recover all the pieces. Raul tells him he needs to make an emergency call to Mexico City. He wants to call his women. He will arrange for them to come. They will be here as soon as they hear his voice. Many young girls, he says. 'Jove y duro!' They will drop everything and come running. They know their life is useless without him. They will be of all colors and sizes. He guarantees me this. They will have willing eyes. Beautiful and willing. They will have hips like a mare's; hair like a horse's mane! Some of them will sing the ancient cantados of their village. Some of them will dance. They will all be willing! The desk clerk slowly stands and presents the broken pieces of the phone to Raul in his open hands. He tells us a call is now impossible. Raul lunges at the little man as though to grab him by the throat but then reels away from him toward the staircase, mumbling in Spanish. We stagger up the stairs and into his room.

He falls on the bed faceup, and I take off his boots. I expect his eyes to close, but they stay open and rolling. He asks me to get his pistol out of the top drawer. I tell him this is probably not a good idea right now. Wait until morning. His eyes become very Apache all of a sudden. They sink way back and turn completely black, with no pupil to speak of. A shift comes over his face, like the sun slipping behind the clouds. He asks me again for his pistol, and this time his voice is very slow and deliberate. It has fate locked in it. I get the pistol for him. It's parked under his underwear, in a hand-tooled brown holster: an abalone-grip Colt .45. Engraved on the barrel are the words *El Indio*. Raul smiles at me when he sees his gun. His eyes begin to return to a world I can recognize. 'Emilio Fernandez,' he says, and points to his chest with his thumb. 'Estoy Emilio Fernandez – El Indio.' I hand him the pistol and he rolls the chamber twice but never takes his eyes off me. He keeps smiling and slowly raises the gun toward my head. He pulls the hammer back and keeps right on smiling. He trains the barrel between my eyes, but I feel nothing. No fear. Nothing. As though there were no border between life and death. I smile back at him. 'What we need is women,' he says. 'Yes? Is this not true?'

'Yes,' I say. 'That's exactly what we need.'

3/10/90 (PAPANTLA, MEXICO)

Winging It

In this scene I'm playing now, I'm supposed to burst into this shack on a run-down tobacco plantation and discover that my childhood friend, whom I haven't seen for twenty years, has hanged himself from the rafters. The 'friend' is played by a dummy, complete with broken neck, bulging eyeballs, phony blood trickling out its mouth and all its skin turned puffy and milky white. Anybody can tell it's a dummy. It wouldn't fool a house dog. But I'm supposed to somehow muster up the belief that this is indeed my long-lost buddy. He bears no resemblance to anyone I've ever met, dead or alive. I've seen corpses, but they never looked like this one. The only dead things I've seen hanging were deer and pheasant. I've been in the presence of death several times, but the memory of those dying ones doesn't provoke anything like the correct response to this situation. Grief is different from horror. I know what my character's reaction should be, but I know if I try to imitate this idea in my head, it will come out being exactly what it is – an imitation. I cast my fate to the wind and try to just wing it on the first take. No rehearsal; just wing it and see what happens.

I burst into the shack and discover the swinging phony corpse, but just as I look up at it, the entire door of the shack breaks off its hinges and slams me square in the head. It's a rude awakening. As I'm recovering from the blow, it occurs to me that this might in fact be a way to approach the moment of the character's discovery. As though he's been hit in the head by a door. Why not? I haven't come up with anything else. On the second take, after the door's been remounted, I try it this way. I wing it. The director says: 'Yes, yes! But it appears to be more physical than psychological. Why is that?'

'Oh, you want "psychological"?' I say. 'I didn't know you were looking for that.'

'Well, "psychological" is perhaps the wrong word. But you know what I mean. Something to do with his torment.'

'Ah, okay. Psychological torment. Okay.'

'Well, these are perhaps not the right words. I just wasn't sure what it was you were responding to in that moment.'

'I was trying to play it as though he'd just been hit in the head by a door.'

'I see. But why? What has this got to do with the situation?' he says.

'I don't know. I thought it might work. I'm desperate for suggestions.'

'Well,' he says, 'it's very simple. You haven't seen your dear friend for twenty years, and you walk in and discover that he's hanged himself from the rafters. That's quite different from being hit in the head by a door, isn't it?'

'I suppose you're right. I don't know. Yeah, I guess you're right. I was just experimenting.'

'Good! That's good! I love experimenting. I'm an

experimenter myself. Just try something else. Are you ready? Are we ready, everyone? Let's try another one.'

'Ready,' I say.

'Good! Camera! Camera! Let's have silence, please! Silencio! We're going to go again!'

On the third take I burst into the shack, the door stays on its hinges; I don't play as though I've been hit in the head by it; I stare up at the phony corpse; nothing happens; I see a prop radio on a bench, and for some reason I stagger over toward it and turn it on.

'Cut! Cut!' he screams. 'I don't understand this either. What is happening here? Why are you all of a sudden turning the radio on? I don't get this.'

'I have no idea,' I say. 'It was just an impulse.'

'Good! Very good. I love impulses. That's the way I love to work myself; instinctually. That's very good. Let's try again.'

'But I thought you said you didn't understand it.'

'I don't, but it's very mysterious. It has a mysterious quality. It might be good. It gives me an idea. What if the radio is already on, and it's playing as you burst in the door. Then you see the corpse and you cross to the radio and turn it off. Shall we try it like that?'

'You mean turn it *off* as opposed to turning it *on*?'

'Exactly,' he says. 'That's exactly right. You turn the radio *off*.'

'That's the only thing you want to change?'

'That's it. Everything else is perfect.'

'Okay.'

On the fourth take, I burst in, discover the corpse; the radio is playing; I cross over to it and just stand there staring at it. The camera keeps rolling on my back. The radio keeps playing.

'Cut! Cut! Did we forget something?' he says.

'Well, you know, I was wondering – I was trying to follow this new impulse that came up.'

'Which one was that?'

'I was just wondering what it would be like to keep listening to the radio for a while, after seeing my buddy hanging there.'

'Yes, but for how long?' he says. 'We can't just keep rolling film on your back. It's not interesting.'

'Right. I see your point.'

'Let's try one more, please. We've almost got it. I feel good about this. I think we're very, very close.'

On the fifth take, I burst in the door; discover my dummy buddy; walk straight to the playing radio and snap it off.

'Cut! Cut!' he says. 'Now, what I feel – what I'm feeling now is that it's too automatic. He just walks over there and turns the radio off as though nothing's happened. There's no reason. It's lost all its mystery now.'

'I felt that too,' I say. 'I've felt that from the very start. A lack of mystery.'

'Well, let's try one more. We're very close now. I can feel it.'

On the sixth take, I burst in the door; discover the corpse; pause for a second; cross to the radio; pause again, then I smash the radio to the floor with my fist. I just cold-cock the sonofabitch.

'Cut! Cut!' he says. 'That's perfect! Absolutely perfect! That's the one. Print this one! It was perfect.'

3/90 (PASO DE VALENCIA, MEXICO)

(Just because they say 'Action!'
doesn't mean you have to do anything.

Marlon Brando)

Tecolutla River

Me and Hendker find ourselves in the International again with him at the wheel. He's very nervous about this truck now. It's not cooperating for him at all. The clutch is barely hanging on by a thread. Today we're supposed to drive across the shallow part of this huge river; make a wide banana-shaped turn; head straight toward the camera; then charge on toward the ancient ferry that's waiting for us by the opposite shoreline. Again, it's a simple enough mission for us, but the background action is complex. There's yet another group of Indian extras on the beach behind us, with fishing nets, who are supposed to move in unison when we pass them. They're having trouble understanding right from left. There's another Indian, knee-deep in the river, who's supposed to wave to us as the truck goes by. It's Raul. He's still sloshed from the night before. That much tequila takes a long time to evaporate. He can barely lift his arm in our direction. His eyes look like a train ran over them. He doesn't seem to recognize me at all. I lean out the window of the truck and yell at him: 'Emilio Fernandez! Hey, Emilio!' He just stares at me in his wet pajamas, then turns back toward the faraway camera, completely bewildered.

Hendker has stalled the truck again, and we decide maybe it's better if we swap places and let me drive. I've driven trucks before. As soon as I climb behind the wheel, I realize what Hendker's been up against. The steering has so much play in it that you have to crank it three times before the wheels even begin to turn. The clutch doesn't engage until you completely release it, and then the lurching starts and continues until it finally finds its groove and levels out. On 'Action!' we get off to a fairly smooth start. Everything seems to be going perfect. The group of fishermen move with their nets in the right direction. Raul manages a limp wave and never looks at the camera. The International lumbers along through the shallow water. Nobody's screaming or acting hysterical around the camera, as far as I can tell. I make the banana turn and head in toward shore. Hendker is 'acting' his heart out even though the camera's six miles away. He's going through some internal thing I can't quite decipher, clutching his knees and grinning madly. Suddenly, I feel the whole rear end of the truck slipping and spitting gravel. We've hit a soft spot in the riverbed. I shift down to second, and the entire back end sinks clear up to the fender wells. The truck stalls dead. Now we're sitting there in the middle of the river, with the nose of the truck sticking up at a forty-five-degree angle and the rear end under water. We must look a little like the *Titanic* just before it gave up the ghost. *Now* there's screaming around the camera. Lots of wild gesticulating. I can see them through the windshield, leaping around like locusts, waving their arms at us. They don't seem to realize that we've stalled. They keep right on waving for us to continue toward camera, as though we can't follow directions or something. I start waving back at them, out the window, but they keep waving us on. '*Cut the camera!*' I yell out, but we're still too far away for them to hear me. Hendker keeps right on 'acting.' I tell him the shot's over. 'We've stalled,' I tell him. 'Nobody said "Cut",' he says, making sure his face stays in character.

'*I* said "Cut", but they didn't hear me.'

'*You* said "Cut"?' he says, grinning like a mad dog.

'That's right. I did. But I don't think they heard me.'

'But you're not the director.'

'No, I'm not.'

'In Europe, only the director can say "Cut,"' he says.

'This ain't Europe, it's Mexico, and any fool can tell the shot's over.' Slowly, his facial attitude melts. He has this facial attitude he's developed already, of fatigue and resignation. I can't tell how much of it actually belongs to him and how much belongs to the character, but some part of its starts to peel away. At least he's got something going for himself. All I'm trying to do is drive a fucking truck across a river, and I can't even get that done. We're stranded alone in this wreck, with the camera miles away. The river surrounds us on all sides. 'Where are you from in Germany?' I ask him casually, since it looks like the two of us are going to be spending some time marooned out here. He seems confused by personal conversation, still reluctant to step all the way out of character. There might be some slim chance the film is still rolling.

'Bavaria,' he says. 'A small village in the mountains.'

'Must be very peaceful,' I say.

'It is.'

'Are you married?' I ask him.

'Yes. Three children. They are grown now.'

'That must be hard. To see them all go their separate ways.'

'Not really, no. My wife and I enjoy the solitude.' He keeps squinting through the windshield in the direction of the camera, hoping for some sign of rescue. Sweat oozes from his eyebrows.

'Do you like acting?' I ask him. He turns to me with a beaming smile. He's slipped completely out of character now. I have the feeling I'm seeing the real man.

'I love it,' he says. 'I absolutely love it.'

'Have you been doing it a long time?'

'All my life,' he says, and his voice takes on a quiet, philosophical tone. His gaze swings back across the river, toward the now abandoned camera. It's a lonesome sight.

'We seem to be forgotten,' he says with a nervous little chuckle.

'We are,' I say. 'That's what happens to actors in movies.'

'I've worked mostly on the stage, myself.'

'Well, at least you don't have to deal with trucks and rivers.'

'No!' He laughs, then grabs his knees again, as though afraid to lose himself completely. 'Do you think we ought to get out?' he asks.

'We're surrounded by water.'

'Yes, well – it can't be so deep, do you think?'

'I have no idea. At least we've stopped sinking.'

'They don't have – how do you say it? – piranhas down here, do they?'

'Piranhas? No, I don't think so. Not here. That's South America where they have those. The Amazon.'

'Ahh! Here they come now!' he says, jumping like a little boy on the seat and pointing at a green truck heading toward us in the distance. 'They've finally discovered our dilemma!'

Raul is still standing knee-deep in the river with his

shoulders slumped, staring toward shore. I can see him in the rearview mirror. He doesn't move.

'That's Emilio Fernandez,' I say to Hendker, trying to get him to turn around and take a look. 'That's him right there.'

'Who is Emilio Fernandez?' Hendker says, keeping his eyes glued to the approaching rescue truck.

'You never heard of Emilio Fernandez?'

'No. Who is he?'

'A national hero. He killed a critic.'

Hendker breaks into a nervous laugh and wipes his forehead. He gives me a quick glance like I might be a maniac, then pushes the door open with his shoulder. He jumps out into the river, waving desperately at the rescue truck. I yell out the window at him: 'People say he was killed by a jealous wife, but it's not true! You can see for yourself! There he stands! Alive as you or me! Emilio Fernandez himself! El Indio!'

Raul hears me and turns around slowly in the swirling water. He glares at me with his dark eyes surrounded by tiny exploded blood vessels. He raises his arm very slowly and gives me the finger, then turns his back on me again. The sun bounces off his thick neck as his chin sinks down to his chest.

3/13/90 (EL PUERTO BARCA DE BALSA, MEXICO)

Colorado is not a Coward

We're in a village almost completely cut off from modern civilization. It lies at the end of a skinny peninsula, the only access being a primitive ferry that makes two trips a day. There're four vehicles in the whole town, two telephones, one radio, and no TV whatsoever. The entire village has turned out to witness the invasion of the movie company. They stand in little tattered groups, holding their children high on their shoulders. They watch us unloading lighting equipment, sound equipment, camera equipment; equipment worth hundreds of thousands of American dollars. They listen to us speaking French, Italian, German, English, and Greek. They stare at our clothes. They watch us exactly as their children watch us: without judgment, with no animosity, just pure amazement. They giggle and point bashfully at the long blond hair of the grips from West Berlin. They stare at the tattoos and rock-and-roll T-shirts; the ADs running in circles, yelling into their mysterious little black walkie-talkies; the director, waving his arms and speaking four different languages; the soundman, trying to set up his Nagra in the shade of a giant banyan tree, unfolding his deck chair and striped umbrella. The tree is thick with long-tailed grackles, cackling and screaming in unison. The soundman removes his headphones and stares bewilderedly up into the horde of black birds. Someone inside a wood-slat shack with a grass roof turns on the only radio in town. A beautiful corridor ballad comes ringing out through the humid air, joining the sound of the grackles and the giggling children. The soundman throws up his hands in despair. The second AD is running full tilt again, across the plaza, toward the little wood shack where the radio is singing. She's yelling in Spanish at the shack: 'Silencio, por favor! Silencio!' The radio keeps singing; the grackles keep screaming; the children keep giggling; the old men keep laughing; the women laugh at the old men; the young men laugh at the women. There is no crying. Not one child in the whole village is crying. The turkeys are gobbling; the pigs are grunting; the dogs are yapping; the roosters are crowing. Not one car is honking. Now the director is screaming 'Silencio!' but the village sings on. Nothing can stop it, not even the movies.

An old charro, astride an even older horse, with its ribs sticking out, stands in the middle of the dusty street, staring at us, with his leathery hands crossed on the saddle horn. The first AD asks him to move on, since he's right in the middle of the shot. The charro beats his old steed on the rump with a frayed shank of rope, then thumps him hard with his bare heels, but the horse only blinks. He just stands there with his ears drooped and refuses to budge. The whole village laughs. The director yells 'Silencio!' The old charro thrashes his mount again, and the horse gives a couple of pathetic bucks, then walks on. The whole village cheers. The charro grins and tips his huge sombrero. The laughter goes on, ringing out into the jungle. The director suddenly changes his mind and wants the charro back. He thinks he might add something authentic to the background, but it's too late. The old man has disappeared into a mango grove, and the ADs can't find him. He's completely vanished.

The camera's finally ready. We're filming a cockfight on the street in front of a dusty pharmacy. Me and Hendker are supposed to walk into the middle of it and inquire about an old friend we've been searching for. The cockfight is for real, except the spurs of the roosters are capped with little leather balls rather than fixed with blades, as they would be in an actual gambling match. A sand arena has been fixed up on the street for the contestants. The roosters are in place with their handlers. They thrust the fighting cocks toward each other, getting them worked up. Our little French focus puller steps into the sand ring between the two Mexican handlers. He's wearing tight Bermuda shorts and dainty black tennis shoes, and he's drawing the measuring tape out from the lens to the tip of his nose in three-foot increments. He places the tape under the nose of one of the Mexican handlers, who's cradling his rooster like a baby, stroking the luminous red and green feathers on its neck. The handler's mouth is full of water. He holds the rooster up, facing him, then spits the water on the rooster's face and under his wings, and all over the little French focus puller, who takes it very well. He's a good sport. He smiles politely at the Mexican handler, who's so absorbed in preparing his rooster that he hasn't noticed the results of his spitting. The focus puller makes a mark with his finger in the sand, right in front of the Mexican, then backs out of the ring, coiling his tape up and smiling the whole while. He makes a humble little bow as he exits and returns dutifully to the side of the camera, adjusting the lens. The Mexican handler looks down and notices the mark in the sand. He has no idea where it came from, but he wants the sand smooth for his fighting cock, so he erases it with the toe of his sandal. The focus puller looks up and notices his precise mark has disappeared. He can't figure it out. He reenters the ring, uncoils his tape measure again, and makes a brand-new mark in the sand, then exits the same way as before, bowing and smiling. Again, the Mexican erases his mark. The focus puller keeps smiling. This time he brings a small stick with him and sets that down as his mark. The Mexican tosses the stick out. Sticks are even worse than marks for fighting cocks.

When the fight finally gets under way, the shot keeps getting interrupted by the drunken owner of one of the roosters. He keeps stepping into the ring and cheering him on. The director tries to explain to the man that this isn't a real fight. It's just for the camera. But the man doesn't understand. He says his rooster, which he calls Colorado, always fights to the death. He's fought him in Texas, in Arizona, and all over Mexico, and he's always fought to the death. It will spoil him for future fights if he isn't allowed to kill his opponent. The director tells him this isn't possible in the movies. It's illegal to kill any animal for the movies. The owner gets offended and scoops his rooster up in his arms. He says, 'Colorado is not a coward!' and stomps off. The director apologizes, but the owner won't allow his rooster to continue under these circumstances. He staggers away, weaving down the dirt road with his proud rooster stuck under his armpit. He's turned his back on the movies.

3/14/90 (COMALTECO, MEXICO)

Place

Me and my oldest son dragged a huge slab of limestone off
the shore of Lake Michigan up to the little cemetery
overlooking the hayfields of Door County. We hauled it with
an old nylon steer rope I had in the bed of my truck. We dug
a trench for it between two red cedars and dropped it in
edgewise, so the flat white side of the rock would face the
morning sun. For over seventy years, my grandparents on
my mother's side had been buried here in an unmarked
grave. My mother had always been bothered about this, so
we were trying to fix it up for her: place a native stone from
the very same beach where her father had built his cabin,
back at the turn of the century. Later that same day, we
brought her up to take a look at it. A little surprise. She
walked around the stone, with her arms crossed softly on her
chest and a worried look in her eyes. She thanked us both
for the effort and smiled. Then she stopped for a while and
stared hard at the two cedar trees, her eyes running up the

shaggy bark to the thick fernlike canopy. She turned completely around and stared across the little gravel path that divided the Protestant side from the Catholic. 'I think it's in the wrong place,' she said apologetically as she turned back to us and nodded toward our mammoth stone. 'It's been such a long time. I'm trying to remember. I know Pop was buried right next to Mother. That's the way they'd agreed to do it. They always wanted to be side by side like that. Of course, it was their decision not to have a stone. Everyone was so humble in those days. I know Pop wanted it that way; just to dissolve back into the earth and disappear. I just can't for the life of me remember. These two trees were so small back then.' I told her we could move it for her easy enough. It just meant some more digging, and we could easily shift it to a new location. But she couldn't remember the exact spot. 'I'm just not sure. I think this must be the Pooles' plot, though. I seem to remember burying Maude here. I think they owned everything between these two cedars. I remember standing over here during her funeral. It's terrible when you get your funerals mixed up.' She walked back a few paces and stopped, then turned facing out toward the shimmering vast surface of Lake Michigan. The wind caught a wisp of her white hair and blew it across her mouth, but she didn't move. She seemed to be staring far across the great water, clear into Canada. 'Yes, I think I was facing east, toward the lake. I'm sure I was. I remember the wind hitting me, just like this. I could smell the water.'

'Well, maybe we should check with the caretaker, Mom. They'll have a chart or something, showing all the plots.'

'I suppose so,' she said, and turned again, facing the birch woods. 'We'd better just leave it like it is for now.'

Almost exactly a year later, we buried my mother's ashes slightly to the left of the two red cedars. We'd checked with the folks who ran the cemetery, and sure enough, our limestone slab was in the wrong spot, so we dug it up and moved it again. It lined up right behind my mother's grave. Everything was in its place now, and we left it just like that.

5/4/95 (SCOTTSVILLE, VIRGINIA)